T0301077

FAST BY THE HORNS

By Moses McKenzie

AN OLIVE GROVE IN ENDS
FAST BY THE HORNS

FAST BY THE HORNS

Moses McKenzie

WILDFIRE

First published in 2024 by
WILDFIRE
an imprint of HEADLINE PUBLISHING GROUP

Map illustration © Femi McKenzie
Author photo © Gee Photography

1

Cataloguing in Publication Data is available from the British Library

Hardback ISBN 978 1 4722 8316 0
Trade paperback ISBN 978 1 4722 8317 7

Typeset in Dante by CC Book Production

Printed and bound in Great Britain by Clays Ltd, Elcograf S.p.A.

MIX
Paper | Supporting
responsible forestry
FSC
www.fsc.org
FSC® C104740

HEADLINE PUBLISHING GROUP
an Hachette UK Company
Carmelite House
50 Victoria Embankment
London EC4Y 0DZ

www.headline.co.uk
www.hachette.co.uk

Salute to the masters that came before us.
Salute to the masters that are among us.
Salute to the masters of the future.

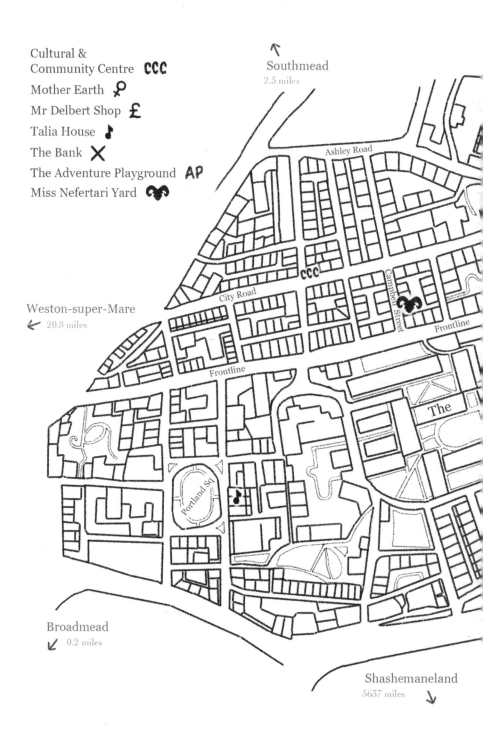

Cultural &
Community Centre **CCC**
Mother Earth ♀
Mr Delbert Shop £
Talia House ♪
The Bank ✗
The Adventure Playground **AP**
Miss Nefertari Yard ♈

Southmead
2.5 miles

Ashley Road

CCC

Campbell Street

Frontline

City Road

Weston-super-Mare
20.8 miles

Frontline

The

Portland Sq

Broadmead
0.2 miles

Shashemaneland
5637 miles

Albany Park

St Andrews
0.9 miles

The Allotments
0.7 miles

Ashley Road

Frontline

Easton
0.4 miles

Map of St Pauls
Bristol, 1980

1

All the story I ever see set off with short dedication that read: *for Jacob*, or *for Mama and Papa*, or, *for all my many brothers and sisters them*, and then everything that come after don't have nothing to do with Jacob, and blast-all to do with any brother or sister. But when I&I story begin: *for Ras Levi*, everything that come afterward – all the likkle things, the tangent, both the present and the past – everything has everything to do with you, Papa. I mean, even when you think say it don't. Because for all this recent talk bout greyness and moral ambiguity, the world is black and white. There is still such thing as right and wrong – plain and simple. No need for complexity or lengthy discussion. No need at all to smoke herb or sit and reason. I know now that what Angela attempt to do that spring of 1980 was right. What I-man done was right. Same with Makeda and Joyce and the rest of the St Pauls people them: the Rasta and the feminist alike. In the end, what all of we done was right. Only you was wrong, Papa. But of course you don't see it that way, you think it's I-man what's wrong, which is where that infernal grey even come about inna the first place. Still, I'm here to show you just how wrong you are. You know some things, a lot of things, but you don't know everything, Papa, so if you do read this, I don't want you fi skip over the things where you think say you know already, like when I start telling you when and where I was born, or how I-man come inna the world, or what St Pauls look like. Because two people, twins even, can see the same exact thing, from the same exact spot – for example a lion hunting a zebra on some African plain – and still come away with two separate account. Which some might say is an example of greyness, but it's not, because there is still a right and a wrong, Papa. The lion pounce pon the zebra and kill it, don't matter if the sun was in one of the twin eye and him see a gazelle, don't matter if the other have bad vision from him born and him see a leopard. Since the Almighty-I is true, there must be a right and there must be a wrong: you taught I&I that, and I won't forget it, even if you have.

So, if you remember, Papa, I was born in 1966, the year His Imperial Majesty Emperor Haile Selassie-I the first visit Jamaica and Rita Marley swear she see the mark pon him hand where Christ was nail to the cross. The stigmata, that's what them call: most people wouldn't know that. Most people never remember 1966 as the year His Imperial Majesty visit Jamaica neither. Them remember it as the year England win the football World Cup. Difference is I don't give one heck bout England. When I was born, it weren't in no hospital. I first open I eye in Miss Nefertari living room, on Campbell Street, in St Pauls, Bristol, not two minutes from the Cultural and Community Centre, not tree from the Mother Earth.

Ras Levi swear him would have a son. Miss Nefertari squat against the wall and never raise her voice. Ras Levi dismiss the local woman from the room and demand I come out in His Imperial Majesty divine name. Then him support Miss Nefertari with him left hand and deliver I with him right. I blink and the first thing I ever seen was the blue tarpaulin them spread fi catch Miss Nefertari blood. The next thing was Ras Levi goatee: long and jungly. Him hand I back to Miss Nefertari, taking such care to avoid the soft part of I head that him let I neck loll and I bawl and bawl. When I was back with Miss Nefertari I did stop and Ras Levi call the woman back inna the room so them could see to them congratulation and irrelevance – induct Miss Nefertari into motherhood, as it were. Then him wash him hand, twice, fetch him tam from the plastic cover arm of the brown leather sofa and went on to meet Ras Joseph Tafari at the top floor of the Cultural and Community Centre, same as him did do every day.

I never ax Ras Levi very many question growing up – it was not the done thing for a boy to ax too much of him fada – but not long before I twelfth earthstrong, I ax him why him did dismiss the local woman from the room, since it never make sense that a man such as himself would partake inna task such as midwifery. Him tell I that it was a lion responsibility to ensure that him cub come inna the world. Him say if I was born an empress then him would've left the sistrens with Miss Nefertari and visit I&I afterward. Him say him would've try until Miss Nefertari did give him a boy: but there I was, him first and only child, and a lion cub was a lion responsibility.

3

I was raise inna household where we might've drank the milk drawn from our goat, but the consumption of meat was as unwelcome as backchat. Where RastafarI language did reign supreme, so I&I did not apprecihate, I&I apprecilove. We did not understand, we overstood. When I was a yuteman I knew all that Ras Levi expect. I would've gathered wood pon the mountaintop of Moriah if it would only contribute to the cause, and when time came, I would plant seed in Shashamaneland for I&I yutes to reap, just like I-man forefather in the hilltop of Jamaica. Ras Levi was our Negus Nagast, our prophet. Him was the first RastafarI in St Pauls when Jah send him from Jamaica in '46, and by the 1960s him had establish and lash RastafarI until the bind could be remove and a brotherhood would remain. Him was a man of presence, Ras Levi – a bronze statue, tall and serious. When the Nazi National Front beat a brother up, it was him one who always march from the centre and muster the troops them. When the coppers did harass a sistren, it was him the people would fetch. A crowd would gather round the enemy and court would be held. It don't matter how many time the pigs them did capture him. It did not matter how many time them flog him inna the street. Him would remain Ras Levi the defence attorney, the patient, the good.

Ras Levi.

Ras Levi.

Him was almost sixty in 1980 but him skin stay satiny. Him seem to be almost sixty I entire life, and sixty may have look old pon some, but him did wear the age better than most man did wear twenty-five. Ras Levi have these narrow, rolling muscle like the Blue Mountain, which stand from him neck and back and ran the length of him arm. Like any Ras, him was as sharp as them come, but him did have a way of turning conversation inna a sermon that make talking to him difficult. You could listen by all means, but him was always going to say exactly what him would've said, whether you gave your twopence or not.

Ras Levi teeth were stain by ganja. Him feature were chisel, and him flaunt him colourful dashiki in the face of Babylon conjecture. When Ras Levi speak, him lion mane shake. You nah affi have locs to be a Ras (it's not the dread pon your head but the love in your heart that make you one of we) but every Ras I ever respect grew them out long. Before Elkanah wife, Hannah, was pregnant with Samuel, she promise Jah never to cut him hair, and him become a prophet. Same way, long-hair Samson was the strongest man to ever live.

It's because of Samuel and Samson that Iyaman grow locs inna the first place, and in the whole of St Pauls, and in the whole of England, Ras Levi were the longest. Them did hang low like ripe fruit and fell to him ankle. Thick in some place and marga in others. In him younger, Christian days, him hair was cut short and was jet black – I'd seen the school photos when him pose as a boy in Jamaica, him face stern, even then, and him collar press – but I remember him mane best budding from a small, greying afro and becoming browner as it grew away from its roots and was mark by the sun. When I was younger, I kept I own locs neat, but after Ras Levi said I tended them like an empress, I soon stop, and them become like his: thick and marga and wild – a crown of thorns.

Ras Levi had Miss Nefertari home-school I-man in I early years. Him care more bout I pan-African study and knowledge of RastafarI than following Babylon curriculum. 'An Englishman can't teach yuh nothing but how to forgive him crime' – is what Ras Levi would say. We never use no book or pen. Ras Levi prefer I was taught like the griot of Western Sudan: everything word of mouth, verbal. That's why I can talk for days on end. That's what Miss Nefertari use to say, anyway. She use to say, 'Boysah Jabari, yuh can talk for days on end, man.' And it's true. Sometimes I talk so much, I forget where I start and affi figure it out by reading the other person body language.

Eventually, and for reasons I'll come to explain, I was send a school age eleven, but still, the only time attendance was compulsory in I&I yard was when I had maths, and that's because Ras Levi say maths is unbias. Him say, 'One plus one is two no matter where yuh go.' And in that him was right, that's why I only excel in two subject: physical education and maths. It's not as if I is a dunce or I have some degenerative mind disease, I can recite Garvey entire life story and most of the King James Bible back to front, but every year I had the most unexplain absence tally in the form register, and the times I wasn't in attendance I would be at Ras Levi hem, travelling for nyahbingi in Handsworth or conference in Moss Side. I follow him to Leeds and Liverpool, Sheffield and Nottingham: learning from the most righteous RastafarI on the island.

Since we never have no secondary school in St Pauls – only two primary, and the nursery the empress them held on the third floor of the centre – we were force to travel miles into Southmead to attend Pen Park Girls and Greenway Boys, or some yutes went into other Nazi National Front area fi them miseducation. Ras Levi did rent a couple bus that took we from Frontline to our respective school gate, but the Nazi soon graffiti them with racist slur and whenever we pass through them area the white boys would pelt the window with rock and mud. It was the same in school. I remember Jim Broad wrote, 'Sarah Beam loves a nigger from St Pauls' on the blackboard, and Mr Fowler left it there a whole ten minute before I pick up I desk and fling it at him head. I was strong like that, always had been. Fowler was in hospital for two day. Them suspend I for ten. Lucky not to see the inside of a cell, some say. But Ras Levi only praise I when the school come and tell him what happen. Him pat I crown and tell Miss Nefertari fi jerk I favourite sweet potato for dinner, with the callaloo on the side and the white rice.

I'm sitting in I borstal cot as I read over this, Papa, prop up by I pillow, pen in hand, amending what I've written these past month. We been inside, what, two years now, Papa? Making the year 1982 and I-man sixteen. An envelope sit atop the desk I share with I celly. The thing already address to your sister prison elsewhere in the north of the country, where you're confine by similar locks and bolts as I: two buffalo soldier label threat to national security, still trap, now more than ever, in Babylon system.

7

You never did respond to none of the other correspondence I sent, and I know that despite the long trial, you may well still be in the dark on the subject of what exactly happen leading up to our imprisonment. I expect you already tell your cellmate that it's I-man fault you're inside. I expect you tell him soon as you reach. And while there is some truth to that, I swear it's not extravagant to say the fault share by Angela, given it was she who start this whole damn thing. But then someone might say it was the one who raise Angela, and then you would affi admit that them would've been mess up by somebody else before them and then somebody else before them, and then somebody would say, 'Well, what bout the English who built and abandon St Pauls?' And once you went back far enough, whether you follow Angela family history, or the English who built and abandon St Pauls, you'd soon arrive at slavery. And since no one want talk bout slavery, and in order to have you overstand why I make the decision I make – the one what land we in here and disappoint you so much – I'll go back to the March of 1980, when Angela come close to blowing the racist bank to kingdom come.

It was one of those maths-less mornings at the beginning of the school week where only Miss Nefertari and I were home – the day this whole trouble start – although of course, I was unaware of its significance at the time. To I-man the day was perfectly normal. I had a stout breakfast of ackee, red onion and fry dumplin, while Miss Nefertari blast 'Look Youthman' on the record player and went round the yard polishing the cutlery and washing the curtains them. She went to work on the kitchen with her buff and wax (of which she had more than two cupboards full), then she let fly at the bathroom and the bedroom them, the living room, the window, and lastly the carpet that ran the stairs. Despite being her one and only yute, in those days I'd never claim to know Miss Nefertari – I had not since a child, and I certainly never did at fourteen. In those days, only fragment of sentence made it from behind her lips. I knew her for muttering, 'It was wrong how them do that,' and, 'Nevermind no bad advice, Missy.' She would tell I to listen as much as I talk, and whenever something go wrong she say, 'God have a wicked sense of humour,' or, 'What-to-do, what-to-do.' When she did speak, she spoke often of divorce, and when she hear tell of Mr so-and-so leaving Mrs so-and-so – because it was always Mr so-and-so doing the leaving – she'd say it was a great shame, a great shame, before busying herself with her music and the smooth ticking of the house.

Back in Clarendon, her mama had taught her that there was no greater embarrassment for a woman than having her man leave. Not long afterward, Miss Nefertari own fada left her mama for a younger woman and the chance of a mistress. And so Miss Nefertari joke would begin and end with Ras Levi imminent departure, quiet half-joke that irritate I fada no end, but she couldn't help herself, so him did learn fi suffer them.

By the time I was fourteen, she had no real bredrin. She kept company and held counsel with herself. She never need a group of tree or no invitation to a mothers' meeting. Her digestion kept her spring. She was tall, still taller than I-man, and compare to the rest of the yutes round the way, I was hardly short. She had locs, same as Ras Levi and I, which she wore garland above her head.

If I remember rightly, she had more to say when I was six or seven. She was more social too. Back then, her voice was deep and gentle, and each sentence went smoothly into the next. In those days her voice kind of purred, not like some back-alley cat, but like one of them rich cats you saw white woman stroking inna the pictures, like a Frenchwoman cat. On the Sabbath, I'd hear her with the other empresses after I'd been sent to bed – sat in the living room swapping song suggestions from LP them did bring to share and talk over. Her friends spoke more than her. I think she like it that way, but them did stop when she start. We all sank deeper into our armchair, or bed, and we lent our ear to the music of her word. She would ax more of her voice then too. She would stretch it on those late nights to sing with the empresses them, and she would use it during the day to shout after I-man or call after a passing neighbour. But at fourteen, I never heard it raise, it was less songful, and her sistren never did come round. She answer the telephone the same way she respond to greetings in the street. She spoke inna manner thoughtful in kind, less she spoke of back home, and then, even for a second, her voice became deep and gentle again, and by time she finish, no matter where you come from, you'd wish you'd grown there too: wish you'd taken your body and flung it, foot over head, into the Rio Minho, wish you'd been raise in relationship with the land. But she never spoke of home when Ras Levi was in the house. Ras Levi look to the future not the past, and Jamaica was the past, so she save it for herself, to be quietly spoken in the inhale and exhale of her morning sigh, times where the centre claim her husband, or the evenings when him did him round, or alone in bed on one of the many night him did spend inna the police station.

Other than talking of home in him absence, Miss Nefertari did everything Ras Levi ax of her, but I knew the community still thought her full of herself. Them wrong though, and I'm not just defending her because she born I – I-man pride I-self on being fair. I know sometimes she did avoid one and two community meeting with claims of fleeting sickness, and I know she had a reputation for cutting small talk short in the street. That I know, and that I can't defend. But I knew that weren't born outta no arrogance, only since I'd come of age, it seem she never care for much beyond Ras Levi and Clarendon.

Even I-man, when the empress did ax after I, Miss Nefertari told them to ax I&I papa, which I admit, if I'd heard another mama say bout them yute, I would've call them petty, or jealous, but coming from Miss Nefertari I imagine she was relieve by it. It was true anyway; I was Ras Levi boy. And I was a man now: I had no reason to take offence, that's just how she was, and I took her as she was; you affi take people how them come. I don't think Miss Nefertari ever dislike, or regret birthing I-man, but relationship adjust over time, and I was all right with that – I swear I was.

Anyhow, it was like I was saying, since she never did much in the way of rest, Miss Nefertari was up cleaning before the sun rise and I&I did rise some hours later, but still before noon. After breakfast, she show I to the lunch she pack for Ras Levi – who, of course, was at the centre – and ax I to bring it him. She put the container inna bag and fill a bokkle of water from the tap. I was soon finding I shoe at the front door. Ras Levi only have two pair of shoe: him steel-toe working boot which him wear in the winter through spring, and would've been wearing then, and a pair of open-toe brown sandal that him save for the English summer. If either became too worn, him would replace them with an identical pair. I only kept two as well: I had I&I school shoe, which double as wedding and funeral shoe too (the circle of life plain in I footwear); and I had I after-school shoe, the same daps I put on that morning. It was nippy out, so I don one of Ras Levi zip leather jacket that hung from the peg beside the door, it had Garvey flag sewn into the collar and sleeve, and hasten from the house holding him lunch with both hand – so the juice from the frying wouldn't spill.

I said everything was nearby in St Pauls and I really meant it: the nearest park was forty-tree seconds away; the shops took fifty-seven seconds to get to, though the journey might've taken someone mampy a minute and thirty-two. The postbox was on Frontline, twenty seconds from I front door, next to the strong lamppost to which the likkle yutes tie rope and take turns in swinging circle. Frontline was a place love by those who never want fi go home. The shops and a green triangular-shape park were at one end, and a housing estate was at the other. Its real name was Grosvenor Road, but only the pigs and strangers call it that. It was a community hub by itself, and we name it Frontline because that's what it was: the copper, arm with them baton and sus law, come into St Pauls by way of it. And when them come, somebody would shout, 'Babylon!', or 'Beastman!', and then anyone who could be falsely accuse of loitering would leave them boombox and them sound system overneath them gazebo, beside the chair and the milk crate them did sit upon, them would leave them meal and board game and conversation and hurry inside, and the yutes would stop playing at the lamppost and the shop shade would slam shut. The pig driver would barely look pon the road when him and him crony crawl down in them bully van and panda car – that's how slow him would drive. Two would stare one way, two another, because them never did come down St Pauls with any less than four. The spinelessness of them number the only consolation for the people who hid from them so often.

2

May Pen Cultural and Community Centre was bang in the miggle of City Road, another of the tree main road in St Pauls love by those who were often outside, where the city remove the bulb from the streetlight to encourage the city badness to migrate and sekkle after dark. It was broad and rich in noise and most of the tall, terrace building had stair and stoop that scale from basement to pavement to front door. When I-man was younger, we did treat the rails them as monkey bar and climbing frame, fit for rough play. Now remembrance grew like weeds round the fracture tile till the place was both City Road and memory lane.

To the unknowing, May Pen Cultural and Community Centre would look like any other house on the long road, but really it was a living piece of history. The red-brick walls of the entrance corridor were line with photograph of the many famous activist and scholar who'd made pilgrimage and paid them respect. The entrance smelt of the fresh paint Ras Levi had the yutesdem reapply whenever the walls were made dirty by children hand and the dust pon the workmen clothes. It wasn't till you went past the lobby that you could smell cook food, and the herb the people them smoke, and the incense we did burn to rid the smell of ganja before it grass we up and bring the pigs them from outside.

We held soup kitchen for the wider community most days, except the Sabbath Saturday. On Sundays we teach class in pre-colonial African history, as well as the Amharic and Oromo languages. I was the best at history and both languages: I could small talk and count to fifty so well you'd never know I wasn't fluent. On Monday and Tuesday there were dance class and stretching for the young empresses and older queens, and martial arts for the man. Typically, you never find nobody good at history, language and martial art, but I swear I'd never lost a fight, and I wasn't one of them yute who think say them can fight just cos them see a couple Chiney flick at the picture.

A non-smoking man name Ras Malachi Femi was the only professional among we, so pon Wednesday him would come and assist some of the St Pauls people with them CV and job application, but since most Ras never believe in no formal economy, and since most of we nah pay no taxes neither, I&I never really pay no attention. When I was of age, if we was still in St Pauls, I wasn't going to get no blasted job in no blasted office and be under some Englishman foot. I was going to be a tradesman, live only pon what I need fi survive – even if some Englishman were to come up to I with him wallet open and offer I one hundred pound to fix the lights in him attic, I'd tell him fi suck out. I was only going work pon West Indian yard. I might work pon a Coolieman yard or a Chineyman yard if times were tough, but I could never work a day for no white man. It wasn't like him want we to, anyhow. Most of we couldn't even pass him telephone interview, speaking with the lilt we have, and even if we happen fi pass, so what? When him see our blackness strolling brazen through him front door, then that, bredrin, would be that. Wednesday was always quiet there at the centre.

On Thursday and Friday we did hand out clothes and medicine to the poorest among Jah people, and we had the empress tend to the sick. I remember a time Ras Levi punish I by sending I fi help the nurse, Sister Kaijah, and you wouldn't never believe the things I did see, iyah: Miss Demarae forward with her son who have one boil pon him thigh; Ras Richard arrive with an incurable case of hiccups; Harrison had a stomach problem and a purple tongue; and Ras Israel wife – I never know her name, but she was a brute – forward straight from the hospital after being discharge too soon. But the thing that upset I most was the state of Ras Stephen. Him was a young man, bout twenty. I remember him best for hosting the monthly quiz. Him was the kind of Rasta who was better with him words than with him hand, so when him come through the door with a nasty smell, bruising pon him rib and glass in him foot, fixing to pass out – I could've put fire to the city council building. Sister Kaijah ax him who trouble him, but I never need to. It was the coppers them, who else? Those low-down, rotten, fucking bastards.

Him tell we how them did pick him up round town and

carry him miles from St Pauls. Them made him step from him shoe, fill them with dog shit, made him step back inside and told him to walk home.

Him never say much through him teeth; only that them would soon pay. The thing with the coppers was you couldn't even get them back like you could the National Front. If it was the Nazi them you could catch them outside them pub and pool-house, outside the mash-up social housing them never look after, but I knew it weren't them: them never have the gall to come trouble we in St Pauls. Them wait fi we fi visit a lady lover in them area, or them take them chance on a night out down town. I knew it wasn't them, but really I never care who it was: if the city weren't going to pay fi it then any Englishman would do. That's just how I felt, and that's what a real man justice was, anyway: taking it inna your own hand.

Jah. RastafarI.

The centre was four storey high, narrow, but it travel back so the space was plenty. The ground floor had a kitchen and a number of wood and metal workshop – everybody in St Pauls was one another handyman. The second floor had studio space for the dance class and martial arts, as well as the mic room for the pirate station. A Ras who went by the name of Bandulu ran it. Him play roots mostly and had guest lecture pon livity and livication. The people enjoy him sound, but Miss Nefertari never play him in her house because him always a interrupt the righteous music to chant down Babylon and send well-wish to far-off member of him ginormous family. The third floor was home to the classroom and the creche, and Ras Levi office and the meeting room was on the fourth and final floor, which was off limit, because that's where the man did discuss, and were even said to keep, the money from our pardna.

Ras Levi start the first pot in St Pauls, and it was him who made sure every Rasta contribute them likkle piece. Even I-man, with I paper round, I took half of it at the end of each week and give it to Ras Levi. Among I papa many name were banker and clerk. It was him vision that made our pardna different to other people pardna, and that's fi two reason. The first is that we never did touch it: I knew people who took turn buying article of furniture with fi them pardna, and I knew more aspiring people who took turn buying rooms in houses and houses whole to break inna flat and divide amongst themself, but ours we left untouch. Which lead I-man to the second reason: we were concern with something far holier than article of furniture and yard; we did plan fi repatriate, back to Ethiopia, the promise land. Not just one or two, but the entire RastafarI community of St Pauls. We weren't like some other Rasta you might come across who um and ah, nor were we like the misguided feminist from the Mother Earth. Iyaman took Garvey prophecy to heart: only in Ethiopia, under a black king, would the black man be free.

Backaday, them people there at the Mother use to see it our way. Them forewoman, a wicked something by the name of Joyce Kelly, use fi assist Sister Kaijah at the community A&E, but, some time before I were born, she went to I papa and complain bout the so-call 'exclusionary expectations of womanhood' in RastafarI. She give RastafarI an ultimatum – either

19

we could fix it, or she would take those loyal to her and float her own group. Of course, Ras Levi told her that there was no place for woman-hater in RastafarI – ours was a way of peace and livity for all black people – but Joyce soon left anyway, splitting the black family and doing the white man work fi them. Ras Levi call Joyce a woman hungry to be a man. Him say that the roles given to man and woman were divine, not subject to time, given by God not man. So when Joyce depart, Ras Levi tell her that she take issue not with him but with the Almighty-I.

The two parts of St Pauls kept mostly apart: to I&I them did lack both purpose and God, and to them we was idealist, hole up inside our centre, ignorant to the true need of the people. But that wasn't true at all. We had Rasta, and the sons of Rasta, station all throughout St Pauls, which was how we even come to hear bout Joyce right-hand, Angela, and her plan fi the bank.

Our receptionist, Sister Ettie, or Sister Dorothy depending on how you knew her, buzz I-man into the centre when I arrive with Ras Levi food. The coat rack was empty. The bare brick in the entrance made the place as crisp as the outside. She reply, 'RastafarI,' to I, 'Selassie-I.' Sister Ettie was old when Ras Levi was young. She tell I that Ras Levi was up top and offer to call him down, but Ras Levi couldn't stand being disturb. 'No, thank yuh, ma'am,' I said, bobbing I head, she ax a dunce question but we weren't nothing without manners. I was bout fi rise upstairs and check Bandulu, when behind I there suddenly came a great fuss as someone ignore the intercom and bang them fist against the door. I check the peephole. It was Denton, Ras Joseph Tafari son, so I wait a likkle longer.

People always a compare Denton and I. We were the same height, same weight, same age, born the same winter month, though him was born in the Bristol Maternity Hospital on St Michael Hill. Everybody always assume we were the best of friend – in school the teacher even call we each other name. Him was softer than I was, though; it nah matter that him locs were longer. And him did have a bad case of eczema all pon him neck, and overneath him eye, pon the back of him hand, and in him elbow crease and armpit. I remember when we was likkle, him use to bawl bout it; saying how much it trouble him, and him mama wouldn't let him out some days because it was so bad, and she affi oil him up with layer and layer of some special white cream and wrap him in bandage.

Some of the yutes in St Pauls use to try tease him, but Denton could throw a punch, and since we was both Rasta, Ras Levi made I&I fight beside him as well, so the teasing never last long. Still, there were looks and some girls said some nasty things. The itchiness make him vex all the time, so him bring it pon himself a likkle, to be honest. Him would even snap at I-man after I back him, so more time we'd end up scrapping too. Him was always more of him daddy shadow than I-man as well. I figure it was the eczema that made him so; him was always waiting for somebody to say something bout it, so him was always screwing up him face, but him would puff out him chest and turn bright when him was round Ras Joseph.

I use to follow I papa all the time too, but where I grew

outta that, him never did. First, a boy was meant to stop following him mama, then him papa, then at around fourteen him become him own man – that's how Ras Levi say life was suppose to work.

Anyway, because of him condition, Denton was always moving and fidgeting, always doing everything inna rush, so I figure it wasn't important, but by time I open up, Denton could hardly speak for catching him breath. Him rest him hand pon him knee, and the eczema overneath him eye did favour one crease bag, and him locs almost brush the floor. Eventually, him manage fi tell we that the pigs them were in the Gardens arresting Angela and that the community was trying to stop them. It was bedlam.

Immediately, Sister Dorothy dial the upstairs line.

'Why yuh never come and tell we sooner?' I say. 'What yuh a deal with, bredda?'

Denton gave I one nasty look while him scratch him arm. 'I got here as fast as I could, man.' Which was true enough: him finish third on sports day. I ax him what the pigs accuse Angela of, but him wouldn't say. Him want fi wait fi Ras Joseph first, which I thought was pathetic. I ax him again, but true to him word him remain hush hush till Ras Levi and Ras Joseph Tafari appear from the fourth floor, and then Denton couldn't stop blasted talking. Him tell all of we how Angela had been arrest in possession of explosive and plan for the bank down a the bottom of City Road. The riot police raid her yard and now them from the Mother have them pen inna the playground.

'Babylon plant the things them on her or she really mean fi

mash up the bank?' Ras Joseph Tafari ax, and Denton confess that him never know. I glance at Ras Levi to garner his reaction, ready to dismiss Angela as irresponsible, or cowardly, or whatever language him would use, but really in I whole life I'd never heard nothing so spectacular. 'What yuh think, Levi?' say Ras Joseph Tafari.

I papa stroke him goatee. Him face straight. 'If Joyce seriously mean fi damage the bank then that woman even more concern with fruitless victory than I already know her fi be.' Him turn to his second-in-command. 'It might be a trap fi get I&I outta the centre and inna the Garden so that them can lock I&I up without the trouble of blasting through I&I door.' Him point at two of the older boys. 'Unuh stay here and make sure nobody don't come in when we gone. ' Him march from the door and the rest of we follow after him: Ras Joseph Tafari, Denton, Sister Dorothy and I, everybody in the centre except those two older boy, we tip and pour onto City Road, twenty-tree of we in total, all in our outerwear, all head toward the Garden.

I mostly knew Angela by reputation: I knew that she never belong to the centre, even when the area was one; that bald-head gossip did whisper ill-proven rumour bout her friendship with Joyce; that she help establish the Mother as a hub; I'd heard that, of the two woman, she was the more prone to violence – which now seem fi be true; and her inability to hold liquor was well-known, mostly because the volume of her drunkenness had woken many a resident, many a time. I knew that she was a product of the children home pon City

Road and had tree fully gold teeth; and I'd heard that she once work there at the supermarket down a Broadmead but was sack for her temperament.

The bank Angela *allegedly* want gone stand alone at the beginning of City Road, near the corner where Frontline converge on Lower Ashley: another of the area lightbulb-less main road. It had a car dealership and a corner store on either side, but it remain detach – too full of itself to associate with any neighbour. Dust spiral inna the lobby. Its desk older than the area. It was red-brick where the other building in St Pauls were white or grey. Its clerks English, its manager and money too: I don't know a single person in St Pauls who keep them money inside; only strangers rush through the doors and pass its watchmen in the foyer. Coppers patrol nearby, them detail double after dark and them German shepherds were without muzzle, and mercurial. At teatime, the few West Indian who ever attempt fi get a loan share story and spin them embarrassment into anecdote to laugh about over Ovaltine and milk biscuit.

We never pass the bank on City Road. Instead, we went down Campbell Street and across Frontline – where the sun always felt warmer. And Denton say, 'Baba, somebody say them see the copper bring fertiliser and oil from Angela yard, the kind yuh use fi make an IED.' I roll I eye. The only reason either of we knew what an IED was, was because every Rasta in St Pauls follow the IRA report. 'Proper,' is what Ras Levi would say whenever the newsman mention them on the radio. 'It's not our fight but them proper still,' him would go on.

'Them nah stand a chance of winning, Jabari, but still them a fight the fight. Them nah have a hope, because them a fight people who favour them, overs? Yuh can't tell a English from a Irish till him talk, and an English spy can master an Irish accent, but them can't step inside no black skin, iyah."

We arrive at the edge of the Gardens with Ras Levi still leading the way. The name sound fancy, but really, them were a pebble-dash maze. Nuff low-rise maisonette where the poorest people in St Pauls live. The twisting pathways were crack and without signpost. The walls were top with green-bokkle glass, and if you hadn't grown up playing there you wouldn't be able to orient yourself at all. That's why the rudeboys and the sticksmen hang out there: so them could snatch chain and wallet, and be lost. Even if you live in St Pauls sometimes you did affi be careful in the Gardens, but that was dependent on who you were, I suppose: I was cool with the rudeboys and the sticksmen because them mother often come inna the centre fi food, so them did carry a certain level of respect fi Ras Levi.

The rudeboys and sticksmen, with them suit trouser and trilby, were the first people we did come across as we pass overneath the steel archway that separate Frontline from the housing estate. Them were perch pon people wall, either side of the walkway, smoking the ganja we sell them. A couple of them had the local newspaper hanging from them back pocket. Others had them wide-eye baby pon them lap as accessory. I could hear raise voice and curse word coming from the estate behind them. I thought them might've been in the miggle of things, but then I member say most of them were on the run for minor offence, and the rest never need any more problem with the beastman than them already have.

Them hail we as we arrive and point we toward the playground. We continue through the twisting, oxbow passages, passing Angela empty maisonette. Her front door was lame and open. It wood twist. The pigs had smash the panel glass.

With each step the faraway voices grew louder. I could soon make out the anger of the people separate from that of the police. We turn a corner into the central square where we found a mass of people between we and the playground. Most part when them see we coming, but wherever we travel in any number our reception was mix. It was a sight to see: Iyaman in colourful dress and long hair, walking with our head held to the sky. No one was prouder or more righteous than I&I, but it was no secret that some of our fellow African try diss we; even in Jamaica there were people who would see harm come to RastafarI, all because them was desperate to be involve in the presiding colonial society, and we weren't. The sell-outs see we as troublemaker, rabble-rouser, but we only made trouble where trouble was require: RastafarI never compromise.

Those in the Gardens who recognise the power in our unity pat Ras Levi back and praise Christ Jesus, likkle boys and girls gambol after I&I, and from them porch mamas wave them dishcloth and rag, each with one hand in the air, the other on them hip. I spot Miss Francis, standing impassion pon the roof of an abandon Allegro. The family car had been left fi so long that it was half sunk into the yellow grass, providing regular driving lesson for the local yutes. Miss Francis was a respectable woman, Ras Levi said so, cept for when she drop leaflet through the people them door, calling for a boycott of the ballot. She was too involve in English politics for RastafarI liking, because when one break the word down, politics becomes poly ticks, and you'll find that poly mean many, and tick is a parasite. There is no freedom or song to be found in politics, only disease.

Rumour have it that Miss Francis was once a member of the Labour Party, and that she was ax fi leave fi reason unknown. Her green headwrap was tall and her Christian skirt brush the car roof as she deliver a sermon in her rough, small-island tongue: 'All day long the whole of we complain to the pigs bout the pigs, to the council bout the council, and to the prime minister bout him own cabinet, but we must shape our own destiny!'

As we drew closer to the playground fence, the crowd became more hostile and we saw a number of feminist from the Mother Earth, but them was too preoccupy with the pigs to pay we any mind. I never see Joyce.

'The skinhead nah go nowhere, boy,' Miss Francis continue. 'Take a look, them all round us in them police uniform.' We barge our way to the front, and it was there we first see the coppers, dress in full gear, catch between the swing and the seesaw. 'Whether it's Labour or Conservative, them hold a sham, two-party election every five year, but capitalism is the true ruler of this here country. The pigs aren't nothing but a group of white man employ fi carry out terrorism against the working class, and it's our people who suffer first and most!' The people who listen did shout in response, and at the same time I catch sight of Angela in the playground. The copper had her pon her knee, holding her collar like them hold them dog. Her head had fallen limp pon her clavicle. Her eye and cheek bruise. I voice rose with the rest of the people and we cuss Babylon for all eternity. The uproar sweep I&I along in the rawness of it emotion, and I surrender I-self to the upset.

Denton jab a finger into I rib and Jah know I was ready to box him, when him turn and gesture across the way: there was our classmate, Makeda. Stood pon a short wall, she swung from an empty lamppost, a piece of a blunt in her mouth, smoke rising above her afro. She was wearing a beige jumper overneath her oversize suede jacket, with black trousers and black shoe; dress for a more peaceful occasion than this. Still, it was she who was most comfortable. By her expression alone you would never have known the drama what surround her. She swung easy. At one with herself and her environment. Knowing her to be in the know, older people did tug at her trouser leg and ax her things and she respond as them equal, without deference. Them watch her as she spoke, listening, but her own eye never left the playground.

Makeda hung out in the Mother Earth, so I figure, like the elders had, that she must've known what was really going down. 'She must know what Angela was gonna do from before,' Denton say, reaching the same conclusion as I had two seconds later. 'Rass,' him breathe, 'then it must be true, boy: them was really gonna blow up the bank.' I ignore him and wait for him attention to return to Angela, pretending like I never business, before I slip deeper into the crowd and went to Makeda side.

3

Makeda drop from the wall when I arrive. She took her reefer from her lips and plant two kiss on I cheek – right and left. 'Yuh see what them do Angela, Jabari?' she say. 'The buggers slap her up, man. That's why the neighbour come grab we from the Mother: cos it was kicking off big-time.' Quickly, she return her spliff to her mouth. 'Me know say Angela was swinging tump, though: she wouldn't go down without a fight, man.' She flick a lighter at its end and took a drag.

'Was she actually gonna do it?' I was still alive from when first I hear the news, and the atmosphere only further stoke I emotion.

Makeda made a face. 'Only she and Joyce know for sure.'

'Was she gonna blow it up with the white people them inside?'

'I don't know. What's Denton looking at over there? I'll mash him up, man.'

'Which one yuh reckon would've had a bigger impact – if it was full or empty?'

'Me nah know. Angela would probably plan it early morning,

31

yuh know, or late at night, when everybody asleep in them bed.'

'What bout yuh?'

'What bout me?'

'When would yuh have done it?'

Makeda look pon I. 'Drop it, Jabari.'

'I'm just axing.'

'Drop it.'

'Joyce nah come?' I said, scanning the area. The square was still filling up, despite there not being no room to move, but the people was climbing the glass-bokkle-top wall and finding way to squat atop them. Homeowner let stranger occupy them front garden. And everybody was shoulder to shoulder. With the way people were pushing and shoving, eager for space to breathe, I was sure one and two fights would've flare up another time, specially with so many of Joyce woman and we Ras about, but not now, not with our common enemy in front of we.

Anyone who met I eye did nod, them own eye full up of upset and rage, and I did nod right back. I fed off them feeling and in turn them did feed off I-man.

'She back inna the caf; if she did come the pigs would've grab her fi certain.' Makeda say. Her eye was calmer than the rest of we – she was studying the pigs. 'Levi here?'

'Yeah man, him nah afraid of Babylon, see him over there.' I wave a hand in the direction I'd seen him last, but him was gone, and by the time I turn back, Makeda attention had already wander. She was like that, though, she'd rather be a part of history than hear bout it, and if there wasn't any history to be a part of then she would look to create her own. She was all bout moments, moments; she chase moments like some people chase material things.

She was raise in the centre, same as Denton and I, but she never stay long after her papa went to breed one English woman down a South Bristol. Pretty soon she cut her locs and her fro take shape, and now she have nuff half-caste sibling. Makeda mama, who sometime still cook food there at the centre, forbid her from seeing her papa, but I knew Makeda still saw him. She say her new brothers and sisters them need her inna them life. She act like she don't business bout her mama and papa being separate. She act like she never care him was there with a white woman. But I knew she did.

Enoch was Makeda daddy name. Him was Ras Levi main man before Ras Joseph take him place. Now Ras Levi treat any mention of him like a cuss word and him ban him from St Pauls. When Enoch left, the yutes in the centre behave funny round Makeda, then them completely cut her off when she took them scissors to her locs and start running with the feminist them down at the Mother Earth. But she and I was always more than cool. When she was there, Makeda was the most interesting yute at the centre. She was serious. She could talk as much as I could when she got going, which sometimes made our conversations less like conversations and more like battles, competitions – with the two of we vying fi snatch the other attention.

'Whether Joyce ax her fi do it, or whether the pigs plant the things them on her, Angela is a fool,' Makeda say, the growing passion of her words undermining the coolness of her gaze. 'We don't have enough manpower at the café as it is, without this jankrow going and getting nicked. We got so much we need to do as well, you know? Pearl want start up a theatre workshop, Miss Francis want start one politics class. Everybody and them mama lining up with suggestion and things them want run: somebody need fi oversee all that. Joyce can't do it herself, man, she already doing too much as it is. Angela selfish, getting caught like this. Angela a damn fool.' Her words were harsh, and I hadn't seen it before, but in the hand that never carry her cigarette she was holding a brick – most likely lift from one of the nearby crumbling wall. I realise she care more bout Angela than her insult let on. And she certainly wasn't calm.

Makeda kiss her teeth. 'Now Joyce is gone be inna bad mood and me can't deal with that right now, man. Me swear me can't deal with it.' We stood there, Makeda smoking her likkle blunt and I-man watching the swelling people, and we carried on standing there till the coppers eventually made a break for them panda car.

It was bout the same time Makeda finish her smoke, so her attention was nowhere else. The pigs haul Angela to her feet, and I hear Makeda say, 'Here we go, boy,' overneath her breath, bristling and poise like Queen Muhumusa. I could see Angela face more clearly: it was mark and cut. I cup I hands to I mouth and shout that the criminal would pay fi them sin, if not in this life then in the next. Makeda look pon I, her black eye sun-dancing, and she swung back onto the lamppost.

The people jostle as the pigs beat them way through the thicket. Them surround Angela like say it was them protecting her from us. Them did hold her up, her feet a likkle above the ground, and them keep her in the miggle of them Roman formation, ushering her through the centre of the Gardens, but faithfully the people follow them, those from the Mother, the regular folk and Rastafarī too. Them left the gardens in which them had found space, them drop down from the walls. Them surge. The people catch inna the miggle get crush but together the people them move forward. I'd lost sight of I papa but I knew say him would be amongst it somewhere. I turn and see even the rudeboys and sticksmen left the safety of them perch. Them left them baby with them babymother, and were pushing through the chaos toward Angela. Them make good progress too, more progress than anybody else, so Makeda leap from her post and together we move with the rudeboys and sticksmen until we were almost within striking distance of the pigs charge with covering them retreat.

Them was farm-boy mostly: the coppers who walk the beat through St Pauls. Ras Levi said the city recruit them from Somerset and Gloucestershire, place them could've spend them whole life without seeing a West Indian. The pig at the back of the procession was no different from the rest: blond hair and baby blues overneath him helmet. Ras Levi always say the smart Englishman find job in accountancy or law, it was the dunce who become pigs.

I dry the sweat from I hand against the cloth of I trouser, thinking bout murder, and it was then I felt Makeda slip away.

35

She never go far, only a half step, but I did turn in time to see the whip of her arm as she dash the brick and watch as it take an officer from him feet to the ground. The people let loose one roar, and for the briefest of moments I felt I could've lift Makeda atop I shoulder and champion her the whole day, but when I saw the pigs bearing down on I-man with them baton raise, that same elation die in I throat.

I lift a hand to prevent the inevitable, but still them struck I down, them boot flattening I head into the cold concrete. I could only see outta one eye – the other went foggy – but straightaway I knew that them had mistaken I-man as them assailant.

I heard Makeda shout that it was her what done it. I saw the rudeboys' hats flying and them pin in the air as them wrestle with the coppers – who'd seem to multiply, as them always did when trouble happen – but it was of no use. I couldn't tell you how long I was under, but eventually there was enough of a break to catch a glimpse of locs swinging and I heard a powerful voice. Then the stomping stop and two hands hook overneath I armpit and did yank I to I feet. The same hand that lift I, smooth I locs, and the voice ax if I was all right. Once I sense return, I saw that both the hand and the voice belong to I papa. Ras Levi held I head and snap him finger in front of I face. 'Jabari,' him say, 'Jabari, yuh all right, Idrin?' I&I vision was hazy, I hearing shot, but I nod same way. I try smile and tell him all was bless. I seen him face relax, seen the worry crease him feature less, but because Ras Levi was focus on I, because him back was to the coppers, him never see them come. I try stop the batons as them did fall desperately upon him crown, but the sheer amount of people and the violent changing of the black tides meant I couldn't do nothing but holler as the pigs beat him senseless and drag him toward them car. And, for all the people effort, them manage fi take Angela too.

Once them gone, the disturbance quell and somebody start running Marley from them yard. Babylon was chant down and freedom was proclaim. The music carry out over the top of the Garden walls and into the greater area. But it never move I-man. Marley felt too optimistic after the pigs had come and gone in triumph. I sat alone pon the swing holding wet tissue paper to I face and spitting red into the grass, mourning Ras Levi. I watch as the non-residents siphon from the many exits of the Gardens, and as the residents come out from them yard to gossip in them long frock and skirt and them bonnet and them jeans and them Samba shoe and them two- and tree-piece suit of tweed and cotton. Each one of them head was cover by some form of hat, and everybody become one expert on current affairs and them had both the insight and remedy for the plight of all black people worldwide. Whenever there was some commotion, it was the same. Everybody look for somebody who hadn't been there so them could recount exactly what happen with them own spin.

At the same time, nobody want be the person who miss out, so what you were left with was groups of people all round, sometimes in fours, sometimes in fives, some over by the playground, others in them front yard, and them did all chat at once, claiming to have seen things the other never. The threatening grey overhead and the smell of rain wasn't bothering the sunny islanders no more. The same people who would often complain bout them boiler inability to fight the English weather were congregating in the miggle of the Gardens to gossip. Once them found them was unable to impress one group, them simply wander to another and start over. By time them finish I knew no one would be able to agree on what had taken place. Still, in I vexation I did sit and listen, specially to the tree elders stood a short distance behind I.

Each of them had live inna the Gardens the past thirty years: the first was a one Miss Cornwall, who let everybody inna the community raise fi her yute; the second was a bowler-hat-wearing man name Battersby, who outlive him peer only to play the organ at them funeral; and the last was Battersby one bredrin, Mr Henry, who refer to him woman as *the wife* and had her sit in the back of him vehicle when him drive. The tree of them stood inna tight circle, and them think, like all elders think, that because them was only addressing one another, only the tree of them could hear.

Miss Cornwall: See the trouble with fighting the white man is exactly that: yuh can't beat him, no matter how much yuh twist yuh face, no matter how hard yuh bunch yuh fist. We're stuck living inna white man world. That's how God want it, and so that's how it is.

Battersby: That's why I stay outta things, Miss Cornwall. Me, I am a simple man: on Thursdays I collect my cheque down a Godwin House, and the rest of the week I keep myself to myself. Me let the youngsters go bout them business with the coppers. The thing with trouble is yuh don't affi look hard for it. Trouble will always find yuh. So I say just keep inna yuh yard and mind yuh own damn business.

Mr Henry: Now Battersby, it's all very well for yuh to say that, but the only reason we can do that is because the police look at the tree of we and don't see no trouble, and trouble is the word. Them see tree people who soon dead. Them know say we're too old to be thinking bout anything like revolution. We're too old to do anything at all. Just this morning I did affi pull the wife from the bed cos she say her limbs weren't listening to them instruction, none at all. Now yuh tell me how me and the wife could cause the beastman any trouble living like that?

Battersby: That's not age, star – that's the mould inna yuh bathroom.

Mr Henry: Shut yuh mouth, Battersby.

Miss Cornwall: I don't know what's wrong with all of the younger generation. All this talk bout 'colour this', and 'colour that', 'woman place in society', all this fighting police officer and putting explosive inna the bank. What's the bank ever done them? Bank keep people money. Bank never harm nobody. It all start with these Rastafarians, them get all in the yutesdem mind and mash up them head, create trouble where trouble isn't. And that there girl Angela need fi stop bothering herself with who colour and who white, and she need fi start think bout having some pickney before she can't. She getting on. Trouble is, she don't have no mama or fada to speak no sense into her life and tell her that. That's the trouble. She raise in the care system from a child. That's why I for one don't surprise when she come and try something mad like this. A child raise without them mama is a backwards child, yuh understand? A child destine fi trouble. If I was her mama I'd tell her fi sekkle: take time, baby, understand that things are the way them are because Jesus intend them to be; if Him intend things to be any different then it would be so. Yuh can't argue with God. Look what happen to Jonah – him get nyam. We colour people who have suffer on this earth will find reward in the next, amen, that's what my mama taught me, amen, and that's what's right. And don't me start bout Levi, man. Rasta cause trouble everywhere them go. I don't have no time fi them. It's all that ganja them a smoke. It change up, change up them brain. Look, see Levi son there on the swing. Don't look too much 'fore him notice. Battersby, look – see him there. I bet him follow after him daddy and turn mad from cannabis already. What business a child have smoking spliff? What business him have?

Battersby: Levi all right, man.

Miss Cornwall: Levi a troublemaker.

Battersby: Yuh remember the trouble back home in '34?

Mr Henry: Lord, now that was real trouble.

At the mention of Ras Levi and 1934, I clench I fist and feel the heat rise inna I face, but still I never turn. Every yute in St Pauls was well use to having elders, relations or not, speaking bout them right in front of them face, or in I&I case, within

40

earshot right behind I back. And the *trouble* them was talking of was the labour unrest, where tree black coppers beat Ras Levi mama, I paternal nanny, to death in the street miggle. Day after, I grandfada carry her back to Wood Hall, where her people come from, and after him deliver her body back to them, him take him a piece of rope and hang himself in the breadnut tree behind them yard: so the story go at least. Ras Levi never did tell I the tale himself – Miss Nefertari did – so as far as I papa know, I never know nothing bout nothing at all. I did play the dumb fool, same as I was doing now. People better told you who them were that way, anyway.

Miss Cornwall: Christ burden we with what we can bear, Battersby. Don't forget, it was my mama sister who live next door to him family in May Pen, so I remember him, him mama, him daddy too, and the whole of them was mad. My mama tell me Levi daddy always a talk bout unfair wage and unfair working condition. She say everybody else got on with them life but unfair was him favourite word. Deep down the man was wockless. My mama tell me it was him mouth what get him woman kill, and the others who get injure at the march, too. So no, I don't feel sorry for the man Levi – not one bit. After him parent pass, I use to hear all sorts bout him. How him always a run from A to B, him never a walk; him never have no shoe or no shirt on neither, even in church; how him a fight people pickney inna Sunday School, fight people dog and him a climb tree – that boy was more monkey than man before him ever come a St Pauls – then all of a sudden, him want grow out him hair long like woman and follow after that jankrow, Haile

41

Selassie. That man was not Jesus! Him just a man: that's why him dead and him never come back. Him was a stupid man as well. Rastaman love talk bout strength, but them forget that Haile Selassie fled him land and come live inna Bath – Bath! My mama use to tell me yuh always affi watch for people who find religion too quick. Yuh shouldn't enter into no relationship with God at a time of too much emotion; never go in too happy or too sad, baby; if yuh do, then yuh likely to leave soon as yuh circumstance change. She say it's the first sign of madness – if yuh rush to religion you'll rush and miss God.

Mr Henry: The whole affair sad when you really break it down and examine it.

Miss Cornwall: Course it sad. Levi raise himself, Angela raise herself, it's no surprise them turn out like this if yuh ax me. No surprise at all, if yuh ax me.

Mr Henry: Well, nobody axing you, Cornwall.

Miss Cornwall never reply.

Battersby: Whoever Levi was back in Jamaica, we can all accept that him come from tough beginnings. If anything, Henry, him make more sense than Miss Joyce and Miss Angela, lovely ladies though they are. Them want change up everything them don't like bout England till them make it inna country full up of colour people. Well, if yuh nah like it that much then leave, star – that's what I say. There's plenty a colour people country in this world, at least Levi know that.

Miss Cornwall: But why Rastaman ever come a England if them hate it so much?

Mr Henry: All of this funny business make yuh wonder

how him son will grow, don't it? All my years I never see my papa get lick down by nobody. I born thinking my papa the strongest man that ever live, and I think the same thing till him drop down. That's what a boy need. Think how many time that boy's seen Levi mash up. Unuh can't tell me nothing, that must do something to him head.

Miss Cornwall: The boy turn mad already. Yuh don't hear how him dash a table at him teacher a while back? The boy don't right, man; him inherit too much anger in him spirit and it all a bubble up inside him, just like him daddy.

Battersby: Levi all right, man.

Miss Cornwall: Yuh only saying that because yuh nyam food at him place, and yuh only eat there cos yuh spend too much. Champagne life on a lemonade wage – ain't that right, Mr Henry?

Battersby: Quiet, Cornwall. Don't mind my pocket, mind yuh own. I've got my money.

Mr Henry: This here will end in disaster; I've seen disaster many time.

Again, I spat blood at the ground pon the grass and I ignore Miss Cornwall gasp and the subsequent mutterings it cause. One whole side of I face was hurting so much I almost forget I manners; Miss Cornwall were lucky I never turn round and cuss her to rass. The only thing that kept I-man from doing so was the certain knowledge that Ras Levi would hear bout it when him come home.

Across the way I spy Denton, still at him fada side, but neither him nor him papa did notice I, praise be, because I swear I couldn't be done with seeing Denton mark-up face, and nor could I be doing with Ras Joseph well-wishes neither. Him had always been there, Ras Joseph. For as long as memory serve, him had been there, and it wasn't an exaggeration to say that, ever since Enoch left, him whole personality could be summarise by the number two. When I say that, I mean there wasn't nothing impressive bout him. Him was never cut out to be a natural-born leader like Ras Levi. If you had ax Denton I'm sure him would've list nuff things, but I never see them, and I'm pretty sure no one else did neither – not even him locs was long.

From I perch on the swing, I did watch as him waft through the people. The people ax him what was going to happen – whether him would be able to get Ras Levi outta prison. Some of the Mother Earth people confer with him and offer them sympathy, and I watch him revel as another man for whom I had only contempt did approach him. This man name was Friday Asare. Him was a baldhead who'd move to the Gardens two years prior, him, along with him backwards son: a class-mate of Denton and I at Greenway. Friday newness hadn't stop him from already familiarising himself with all things disreputable in the area. I often seen him in the early morn-ings, when on I paper round, walking back from the clubs in Portland Square, always liquored and in the arms of some English woman. Him wasn't a Ras, and him never frequent the Mother Earth – but for them occasional celebratory lock-in. Him was the worst of St Pauls, always off somewhere with him head inna the sand. 'Day-by-Days' Ras Levi call them, people like Miss Cornwall and Battersby and Mr Henry, people who took it easy, happy leaving both the thinking and the action to the rest of we.

I watch as the two man meet and greet one another, and I recall I introduction to Friday Asare. It was at a community meeting, the topic was regarding *The Black and White Minstrel Show*, which broadcast pon the BBC. At the meeting end, while the discussion still a go on, Friday, who was unknown to most of we then, stood up and argue against Angela, who want the show gone. Him compare the programme to the statue of Edward Colston in the miggle of our city, or Winston Churchill in the miggle of London. Him say them was proclamations: England was telling us who she was and what she was proud of. Him insist we shouldn't have her hide herself from us, lest we forget. Him say it the same way I come fi learn him and him son say anything: with a smirk.

I remember somebody shouting and reminding him of his proclivity for the Englishman woman, to which Friday smile and say that if the Devil exist then him was him advocate, and if black man were no longer sexing white woman then him was dead. I remember the hall laughing hard, even Angela smile before ordering quiet, but I never laugh then and I wasn't laughing now. I stood up in that same meeting, right after Friday. I chair clatter down behind I and everybody turn to look. 'Yuh a laugh after him.' I was steaming. Friday sit cross-leg, him face amuse. 'Yuh a laugh after this jankrow and the British Broadcasting Corporation a laugh after we. Even Churchill looking up from him resting place and him a smile too. Everybody a laugh, but nobody doing.'

I doubt then, same as I do now, that Friday son ever answer the door and find Friday lying inna pool of him own blood and making: that him had ever seen the silhouette of a bully van tearing from the scene of that particular crime. Nor did him affi reconcile with the fact that him could never do one single, blasted thing about it. But I had. I'd been force to reconcile I-self with that fact plenty of times.

I spat red again, and the wet tissue a local had brought from him yard was starting to leak blood back onto I&I face as oppose to absorbing it. I cast it aside, wondering if Ras Levi did blame I for getting him lock up – if him love had lessen on the short journey to the station. Makeda appear at I side and offer what I'm sure she thought were kind words of revenge. She took up the swing next to I-man, she plant her feet on the ground and took ahold of the metal chains so it wouldn't move. The swings was so full of rust that them did make a racket and the dirt got all in your clothes. 'It's always yuh papa, init?' Makeda say, and so it was. Ras Levi had spent more than two thousand hours in jail without a single charge against him name, not just in Bristol neither, but in Cardiff, Birmingham, London and Leeds.

I tune Makeda out and carry on studying Friday. Soon, the Rastas left at the rear of Ras Joseph, the Mother Earth lesbian return to them caf, and after a while there weren't too many people left. Still, I did watch as Friday begin another conversation with another neighbour. Him raise him hand when him feel I&I looking on him, but I never wave back.

The nights Ras Levi spend inna cell I didn't never find no

46

sleep. Instead, I watch fi blue light through the curtain and listen for a knock pon the door, for the voice that come fi apologise, come to tell we that Ras Levi was dead from him wound. Him know them did want him in the ground. The CIA kill one of him uncle in Jamaica. We had a Panther cousin go missing in New York. White man murder who frighten him. And Ras Levi was a real community leader, one anoint by Jah and the people both. Him keep our best interest at heart, not like them at the Mother Earth who split the people in two. Not like Enoch, who abandon him daughter for the enemy bed, or like Ras Joseph Tafari, who was too meek to threaten them, and certainly nothing like Friday, who chase after English skirt for sport. Him was Ras Levi the redoubtable, and that shook them no end.

I head hurt like heck. I don't want be one of them man who find himself inna squabble and go on about it, but it was bad. I rip the end of I shirt and plug a piece up I bleeding nostril. A shiver took I-man. Black spot play in front of I face. Still Makeda went on, but on the other side of the playground, not four feet from the swings, I seen a copper helmet and I head clear a likkle. I knew that if I let it be, one of the neighbour-hood yutes would use it as a plaything. There wasn't much in the way of toys round here, so over time the likkle man might grow so fond of it that him would bring it home, and as it become more precious to him, and as other children want them turn, him might only keep it fi himself. Him might polish and clean it. Take it to show-and-tell. When career day came, him might tell him class that him want be a copper. Him white teacher would smile and say it was a proud profession, and she would say that the community need more colour copper, and her smile and encouragement would carry him all the way through him miseducation until him land pon the doorstep of the pig academy. By then, him would be numb to downpression, numb to the words and plight of our people. Him would become a tool of racism like the coconut coppers down a South Africa, or the one who beat Ras Levi mama. Him very existence playing into Babylon wicked attempt to divide and rule.

I couldn't take it no more, I swear: the sweat, the blood. I jump from the swing and stamp pon the helmet with everything I had . . . but still it refuse to break. I reach down and punch it, mashing up I knuckle even more than the officer boot already had, but that never do nothing neither, so I toss it and it bounce harmlessly against the flats and fell to the ground no more than twenty paces away.

Two yutes run over and argue over whose it was.

I felt Makeda eye pon I back, I heard the people conversation pause, I could smell Ras Levi in the jacket I wore. I tore it off and cut out from the area. I hear Makeda shout after I, but even with I body in pain, I was soon outta the Gardens. I ran along Frontline, up past the bank and the allotment, and I never stop until I reach the neighbouring St Andrews.

4

When you first hear the name *St Andrews*, you might think that it was something like St Pauls, being that them were both name after saint, but if I affi guess which was closer to Jesus heart, base solely pon the two area, I would've bet the pardna on Andrew. I'd passed through before, never wandered. Still, I spent the rest of the late morning and early afternoon in the fancy area, looking into homes and over fence into garden, picking up stones from driveway and tossing them up at windows.

Peeping into them life, I realise that white people were more boasy with them love than we were. Them never have no image of the Last Supper pon them wall, nor no map of them island like we had. Instead, them photograph track them yute every achievement from primary school, where them were shot riding pon them papa back, to university graduation and marriage, with them mama arm slung round them, smiling with all them front teeth. It was too much iyah, like them was worshipping them pickney or something – I swear them were so please with themself.

I couldn't remember a time when Ras Levi took I&I inna him fold and hug I-man chest-to-chest. I couldn't remember a time when him tell I him love I-man. Miss Nefertari never had in years, neither. And I'm not complaining; them overstood there wasn't no need. Them did show them love in realer ways anyway; Miss Nefertari cook and clean – take care of the yard, and Ras Levi . . . well, I papa just threw himself in harm way to protect I&I from Babylon. I swear I would much rather be shown love than told some pretty words – I swear I would. But take St Andrews. Everybody in St Andrews seem fi give them yute the bedroom at the front of the yard so them could scrawl, 'I love Mummy and Daddy' pon them piece of sugar paper and decorate them with collage of rainbow and sunshine and stick them inna them window, so when Mummy and Daddy come home it would be the first thing them see, and when them did have guest over them could point the paper out and laugh bout how cute them pickney were. It was all for show. I bet them yute nah feel half the things them express pon paper – I wouldn't even be surprise if the parents them had made the slapdash collage themself.

Them life was easy. That's why them had the time to express themself in words. Words were a luxury of the rich, or the imprison. Nobody in St Andrews never affi worry bout nothing; not finding work, not filling them fridge. I imagine them never have no trouble getting these yards neither. Them was a world away from going fi buy them first property and being told them nah sell a colour. I imagine them all had good job and them was so blasted happy with themself fi living inna

50

place such as St Andrews that them hardly did affi engage them brain at all.

Them had them parking for one and two vehicle and a rear garden too. The people did wear gilet and walk fi them Labrador, them did have uniform milkmen leave glass bokkle pon them step. Them lollipop lady did protect them children, them nah have no panda car stop and searching them. These were the people who use the bank in St Pauls. We see them forward in them saloon and them grand estate. The man left them family out front, and them never get no ticket no matter how long them take. Then them swan back up the hill, where the pavement were line with tree that rain orange leaf in the autumn, and the root of the tree never crack the pavement, them stay in them place, tuck neatly overneath the broad slabs. The people of St Andrews did love the fact that the slabs never craze, and that the leaves turn orange and drop in the autumn, because then them could meet in the miggle of the footway with them dog on long leashes and natter.

Most of we never have no garden in St Pauls; most green-thumb resident of St Pauls affi join a waiting list for a plot in the allotment and did affi strain them back and knee walking up the tall hill because the bus don't often come. Ras Levi ensure him have him piece of land in the allotments. Him always speak bout Adam and Eve, and how Jah intend for I&I to live in harmony with both Him and nature. Ras Levi say that being a farmer was the purest living there was, that once we make it to Ethiopia, we would raise pawpaw and pear, mango, tomato and teff. I can admit that part of living in St Andrews would've been nice; them could keep them likkle herb and tend them vegetable, them could live them life at peace with the natural world still in reach.

I pass a particularly large house with a large garden and walk the alley that ran its side before climbing the fence, just to see. Across the way, overneath the opposite side, there was this great, big, white and brown dog lain asleep in the March sun, trying to soak up what small heat it struggle fi give. I couldn't tell what breed it was, but it was a him. I whistle till him lift him head and come to the fence. Him nah bark and him seem friendly, so I hop the fence and play with him a likkle. Him collar never have no name tag so I name him *Idrin*. If the owner them saw from them window then I'd be back over the fence and down the alley inna second, but I never plan on staying long.

A house and garden in St Andrews wasn't a dream for a man such as I: I had dreams of an Ethiopia far grander.

The dog did roll onto its belly and I gave it more rubs, thinking back to the goat I did rear with Miss Nefertari. Ras Levi had been against I&I getting the grazer to begin with, but in those days Miss Nefertari would occasionally insist upon things, and even more occasionally she might even have her way. She got it for herself as much as for I-man, but that never bother I; she said it remind her of back home and I was glad she could share that with her son.

Pretty was the goat name, on account of her lash, and she was real smart – you could see it in her eye – too smart to be kept in our degga backyard, tell the truth. Pretty would've love a garden like this: it had a lawn and a pave area and she would've chew the plants them in the flowerbed that ring the fence. This was the kind of garden where a mama and her son could raise an animal. The kind of garden that might have a mama and son tend it for long, well into the son teenage years and beyond. It wasn't long before I heard a yute calling for the dog from the yard, and after a final rub, I made myself scarce. I pocket I hand and carry on through the area.

All things consider, I guess the houses in St Andrews were nice, better than the maisonette in the Gardens; the smaller yard round Albany Park; and the medium ones, like the one I did live in. The only thing we had in St Pauls that could compare were the yards along City Road, and even then, the majority of places were split into flats now. There was a time when them had been grand four- and five-storey houses, back when them was own by slave-trader. But, true to them nature, the slavers kept the yards fi themself until the area was shell inna the Second World War – only then did them leave and it did become one of the first reception area for the immigrants arriving to the city.

At first the white landlord keep the big house as them were, but soon them realise them could make more money from renting single rooms and flats. I remember Miss Wilson use to have a full house on City Road, and she need it too: she had nine children before she reach forty – them call her husband Straight Shooter and them call her Oven. She had a couple who were round I age, and outta nine children you would've

53

thought I might've been bredrins with a couple, but they were Day-by-Days.

It was sad what happen to Miss Wilson family home, but anyone who knows anything would've already figure that her landlord wouldn't let them keep the place to themself. Like I said, though, Day-by-Days don't concern themself with the wider issues of society. So long as there was food pon them table and a roof over them head, much like the English in St Andrews, them was happy. Happy with them likkle job and them likkle yard, happy living in England and obeying her likkle laws. But the trouble was, England could never tell the Day-by-Days from the troublemakers – she never want know. So when Miss Wilson landlord want them gone, and when them did refuse, him pay some down-and-out to set the house aflame, and no one never see who it was because of the missing bulb, and Miss Wilson couldn't overstand why the fire service was so slow to respond.

Whenever I think of Miss Wilson and her family, I see flames, like I'm still standing in front of the fire in I pyjama. It was bout nine at night, and the sky was black and starless so it look as though the fire went a mile high, right up to Heaven. And the heat, chuh! If you've never stood in front of a burning house you wouldn't know, but there's nothing so hot. Somebody say it's the personal belongings that make it so – the memories and them things there. The whole of St Pauls come out to watch Miss Wilson yard disappear, cept for Miss Nefertari, who did stay home. I was just a yuteman at the time, so I stood next to Miss Wilson, who was tearing at her hair and wailing, watching the place go up. Even then, we all know say it was the landlord who order it done as well. Him was never lock up, nor was him ever charge, and as soon as the fire was put out, him build the place right back up and separate it inna tree flat as if nothing never happen. Only the Day-by-Days need the justice system to confirm them suspicion, the rest of we, even them at the Mother, know wagwan.

Eventually, that night of the fire, Ras Joseph took on the burden that Miss Wilson had become. Him remove him jacket and proceed to wrap her in it. She held onto him like say him was her baby-fada, but Shooter was down one of the pub pon Frontline. I think that was when somebody start the head-count of Miss Wilson children and we realise that two of them was missing. Yes, it was round that time, because someone had not long gone to fetch Ras Levi from the centre, and him come running down the long road just as the news sweep through the people them. While everybody else did cover them mouth, or pass the news on, or ax where the fire brigade was, or wail, or pray that the yutesdem hadn't been caught in the fire, Ras Levi rush inside, full of love.

I remember it was dead silent after that, and for those few minutes I did forget how hot it was. I soon found myself at the very front of the crowd, wishing that somebody else could be the saviour for a change. Then Ras Joseph appear and put one of him arm round I, and him have him other round Denton, and I think that was when a small part of I&I begin to hate them both. After that the firemen arrive and say them could only stop the fire from spreading to the rest of the street.

Them ax if anybody was inside and I felt everybody heavy eye, but I did ignore them all. I had to believe that Jah would keep Ras Levi from passing in something as plain as a house fire – specially after him beat death so many time before. And when him appear overneath the porch with both of Miss Wilson children tuck overneath him arm, I remember the people cheering and the firemen offering him work and Miss Wilson weeping and I was so proud and relieve that I did tear up too, though the heat soon dry the water, and in the midst of all the congratulation I hear somebody question Ras Levi commitment to Miss Nefertari and I, seeing as how him put himself in danger so often, and I hear another stranger call him too showy: always wanting to impress everybody, and I remember Ras Joseph tightening him hold of I.

In the end, Miss Wilson never did find a home to keep her children together; some went to them aunty, others to them grandparent, Shooter die of cancer in him liver the following year. The St Andrews yards and the tree with all them leaf and unspoilt pavements were impressive, but all I could think bout was Miss Wilson and the house fire and the whether or not I was the foremost object of Ras Levi love. I was forever glad that I was born into Rasta, that I wasn't a Day-by-Day, but if the pigs could beat and lock up I papa, right in front of I, then really I was quite like Miss Wilson: helpless and watching a great fire raze I home.

5

I found a wall to sit on – an end-of-terrace – not long after leaving the back garden, and it was there where Makeda sneak up and give I one hefty shove and I fall backward in the bush. She help I-man back up and declare that I nah affi apologise for running off and having her search up and down, axing people where I'd gone . . . not that I was going to. Then we sit pon the wall together, talking bout the yard them and the people and the car that pass. She told I to stop touching I eye, that I'd only make the swelling worse, and she hand I some more wet tissues that she bring, but the bleeding had mostly stop by then. I told her I could feel the dry blood waiting stale above I lip. I nah bother fi wipe it. I tell her that it make I-man look braver. She laugh and say it was the only moustache I'd ever get. I told her to mind her own, and I glance at her while she went on, but there wasn't much I could diss. Her ears were oversize. Her hair was natural, and she had these black eye, and I mean really, seriously black, not brown like the people who say them eye black but when you look pon them you realise them eye is closer to a dark brown – them was as black as could be. Her face was wide, not fat, but sort of flat and wide, and it was frame by her fro. She had nuff likkle acne scar over the bridge of her nose, except them never stand out much on account of her complexion, which was bout the same brown as I-man, so you only notice them if you were close, and if you were that close, then all you'd be looking at were her two eye. Makeda was always ramping anyway, so I left it.

I gave her some stones to throw, and she broke a window on her first attempt – I tell her she never have no self-control, and she snap and call I-man a bloodclart chicken. Quickly, we set bout relocating to a next part of St Andrews, where we found another wall and sat together gossiping again. She lick her finger and wipe the blood from the top of I lip. She ax I whether Ras Joseph was going to use the pot to pay Ras Levi bail or whether RastafarI would do something as drastic as Angela plan to. I never like talking bout the pardna, even to Makeda, but still I tell her that we sometimes did dip inna the pardna for emergency, like when Miss Wilson yard burn down – Ras Levi set her up inna hostel for as long as it took for her to get back on her feet, but really I thought it was high time we took the battle to Babylon. High time them yute grew accustom to sleepless nights like I was. I ax her if she member Miss Wilson yard burning. She said she did, say she remember seeing I-man at the front of the crowd, but it wasn't long before our conversation get interrupt by siren as two copper roll down them window and tell we fi come off the wall and wait where we were.

The two a them were young – which was a problem. The

older coppers were all right sometimes; not *all right*, but if you did affi choose between young and old, you'd choose the old every time. The young coppers cuff we – as a precaution, them say, and I was so wound up I wouldn't stop interrupting them spiel; calling them pigs and bastards and oinking. Makeda kept telling I to shut up, shut up, Jabari, but I wouldn't. I head was gone, taken by a blinding fury. Them made I step from I dap and roll I sock down to I toe. I told them I'd let them search I-man outta the kindness of I heart, cos if I'd felt like running then there wasn't a copper in the city who could catch I. Them laugh and say *is that right?* Then one reach into I pocket and grab ahold of I weapon. It fit small, snug in him hand, and him stroke it fi a second. Him reach under the bottom of I-man balls and feel them too, and when satisfy, him say, 'Guess it's not true what they say,' and again, them both laugh, and that's when I stop talking. Them lay I&I pon I belly and, try as I might, I couldn't stop the water coming from I eye. I couldn't even wipe it away neither because of the cuff, so I lay there, bawling onto the pavement, I body shaking.

Ages ago, when Makeda was still at the centre, Ras Levi teach we how fi handle copper: him tell we fi memorise the telephone number of nearby brothers and sistrens so we might spread the news, or call for reinforcement. Him say that if we were to be caught unaware, inna place that was foreign to us, to answer the pig question simply and play fool fi catch wise: better to adopt a wooden stupidity before Babylon than provoke him, cept, of course, him never need no provocation. The other copper ax if we were a couple as him massage Makeda titty and reach between her leg. I watch as her eye turn glass and want to know where she went. How she could stay so frigid as him did do as him please. How she never bawl like I-man. Makeda was shape like a grown woman; I could tell the man enjoy himself. 'Either of you two know the black bitch we brought in earlier?' him ax, while him linger, rolling him r's like only the English in Bristol did. 'You two live down in St Pauls, right?' Neither of we said a word. I was numb and Makeda was elsewhere. I lift I head and did search for her black eye. I want to let her know that it wouldn't end here, that we would have our day, because our day was promise. Jah wouldn't abandon I&I forever, and we had already suffer so much.

I want fi tell her that I did love her as a sistren, that this wouldn't change what I thought bout her and that I was there for her always. And for the briefest of moment, she met I sight, I seen her attention flicker down toward I-man, but there wasn't nothing behind her eye; no life, no nothing. Her spirit was at large. She had empty the vessel. The copper tilt her body back and press himself against her backside. Her two eye found the sky as she let her neck loll. The clouds were grey and white. It still smell of rain. Once them finish, them uncuff we and recite the article them search we under. Them say somebody had thrown a stone through an upstairs window, that the owner did call it in. Them never have no proof it was we; them only say it was our own fault for looking the way we did and being where we shouldn't've been, them point at the cuts pon I face and say I was clearly a mischief-maker; and besides, there weren't no other niggers in the area. Them laugh a final time. I hands were slick with moisture, mark and made white by gravel.

'Yuh see, Makeda,' I say, once them left, and I was insistent. I rub I face with the back of I sleeve and push the dirt from I hand and clothes back onto the ground. I try make sure I voice never wobble. I could hear it threatening to crack and could only hope Makeda couldn't. I could've kept silent, she wouldn't've notice that way, but I did affi do something to keep busy. 'That's who white people are, bredrin: them sick. That's why Angela should've burn the whole bank to the ground with the white people still inside.' Makeda never move as though she heard I-man. I could see the life slowly returning to her, in the way she was walking and taking in her environment once more, but her mouth was still press close. 'I don't care what yuh say, man,' I continue unabash, 'because given the chance all of them would've done what them just do to we. What, yuh think say it's just them who put on the uniform, sistren? It's all of them, man. The uniform just bring out them true colour. Them put it on and get brave and puff out them chest like say them a badman and behave how them always want behave.'

The afternoon was still brisk, but it felt good for how hot I was. Neither of we did want to go back a St Pauls, so we walk to a newsagent and Makeda buy we a chocolate to half. It must've been sat on the shelf for the past fifty months cos it was greyish. I glance at Makeda, kept glancing, searching for any signs that she thought differently bout I-man, whether she blame I for what happen, for talking us inna one fix, then not protecting her like how I should've done. I wonder whether she thought I was even more of a chicken cos I did bawl. I glance at her again, hoping that maybe she never see.

'Yuh know what it is?' I said, sucking the piece of chocolate she hand to I-man. It never taste as old as it look. 'It's the climate and them history. Remember Europe was an ice cap in Incient days. Living here bred a harsh and unforgiving people, yuh follow, Makeda?' She never reply, instead, she give her attention to the various upstairs window of the big house we pass. 'All that cold did breed a cold-heart people, sistren. It breed the hate in them. Them hate the earth, resent it for being so sunless over them head, them resent the moon for being so cool, hate themself for living under the two cold lights, so of course them hate everybody else as well. That's how them can go inna the world and do what them want. Member what them say: all of we product of our environment. Most people think that means yuh mama and papa, maybe yuh grandparents, but I'm telling yuh, Makeda, it go way beyond that, man. The sun, moon, plants, trees: all of it is our environment and all of it affect we differently. I-man don't believe in evolution, but I hear some African scholar say white people the way they are because them have more Neanderthal in them, that them less human than I&I. I'm not saying that's a fact, but if yuh check the whole of history, Makeda, only white people put so much into the downpression of people: specially I&I.' I couldn't stop, I never know what feelings I would've been left alone with if I had. 'Europe was the last place to have any civilisation. Africa have bout four golden age before Europe have one, all

62

over Africa as well: East, West, North, South. Even the rahtid Chineyman have them time in the sun. All of we could've done the slavery what them do at any time, but we never.'

Makeda finish her chocolate and push the wrapper into somebody bush. 'There's always been slaves.'

'Not like how white people have slaves, though, Makeda: not base pon skin colour and feature and geography and them things there. Yuh can't show I no other people that enslave family line, Makeda, don't matter what yuh say, yuh can't show I that.' I shook I head furiously. 'I know, as a fact, that white people invent that. Them wicked, Makeda. Only Satan could think how them man think and do what them do. Only Satan. That's why them have it coming. I swear them people there a go receive Jah wrath like no one else, iyah, but in the meantime them affi deal with I&I revenge, yuh with I-man, Makeda?'

'Mmmh,' she say.

After another moment, I swore Makeda to secrecy – I never want no one back in St Pauls knowing what them pigs went on with. I said it was something we would both affi take to the grave. Eventually, she nod and I calm down a likkle, cos I knew she never went back on her word. I ax her how she stay so normal throughout, and she look upward again and admit that it wasn't the first time something like that happen to her. She must've notice the shock that took I face, or seen the sudden stiffness in I body language from her eye corner, because she explain how it happen to most of the woman that come inna the Mother – most of the woman she knew. She say the coppers search them like that, whether them had them wife at home or not. She said it all normal as well, her voice devoid of anger – of anything, really. I said I prefer it when them did steal we inna them van and beat we silly – prefer that to them touching we. While Makeda attention was elsewhere, I put I hand inna I trousers and felt I manhood. On the playground I'd had footballs blasted into I crotch before, and the copper hadn't squeeze it so much as caress it, but the feeling of him hand last way longer than any pain ever had.

I say it Angela fault, Ras Levi and I ending up in the big house, but I could've start this story that afternoon, with the pigs touching Makeda and I, cos it was right after that we first see Irie, although we never know her then; to us she was just this likkle black girl alone inna the road. She was dark, bout Makeda and I colour, no older than six, but she was small, real small, like she never eat nothing her whole life. Her hair was scrape back inna ponytail without enough grease. I call for her to come outta the road. But with the way I look, all beat up and bruise, tear-stain, with shirt and tissue still plugging I nose, I thought she would've taken one look and ran, and I wouldn't have blame her neither. Still she come trotting over.

Irie had the same walk as the yutes in the Gardens. It was kind of jittery, like one leg was driving her forward and the other was holding her back. She had this birthmark pon her face where her sideburn would've grown if she were a boy. It was a few shades lighter than the rest of her skin so it stood out. I thought it was kind of shape like Africa turn on its side, like the horn was in the north and what them call West Africa was south. I thought it was pretty though, like it complement her face, inna way.

'My name's Irie, what's your names?' she say, once she arrive in front of we, and she sound more Bristolian than West Indian. She said it all boasy as well: you know how yutes are. Them think say introducing themself is the greatest thing on earth. She held open her arms like she want fi be hug and pick up. I check over her head but there wasn't no one running after her, nor anyone shouting bout no lost child.

I was just bout fi tell her not to be so friendly with stranger when Makeda lean forward and pick her up. 'My name's Makeda, Irie. This is my friend, Jabari. You're so pretty, yuh know, baby. Where yuh come from? Where yuh parents there?' Makeda had found her voice again.

'That's what I wanna know,' I add. 'Yuh shouldn't be outta them sight, man.'

Irie point in the direction she come from. 'I was with them on the slide in the park.'

'In St Andrews Park? Were you going down the slide fast?' Makeda ax. She was doing that thing where adults speak to yutes like say them is soft inna the head. I hate it cos it wasn't fair on them. People, specially the sistrens, speak to children in that same whiny voice from the moment them born, even before them born actually, from the womb right up until the fun wear off and them could no longer bother, then them suddenly start talking to them like say them a adult. That's why I speak to yutes like them grown from the start: it was fairer that way.

'How come unuh in St Andrews anyway?' I said, and she shrug as if to say *I don't know*. Whenever yute shrug them shoulder it was so exaggerated, them whole body move upwards and them make you feel like an idiot for even axing.

I told her to find her manners before I found them for her.

'Jabari!?' Makeda said, like say I'd done something wrong. She thought I was being mean, but she needn't've said any-thing. I was great with yutes. I raise Pretty up from a kid, and there weren't much difference between a kid and a yute; all you affi do was provide them both with shelter and food. Girls think them being born a girl was enough to make them a good parent. Them think playing house as a pickney make them more mature, but it don't.

'What?' I said, 'There ain't really none of we here in St Andrews. There has to be a reason she round here, surely?'

'Well, we're here, aren't we?'

'Yeah, an look what happen,' I said. I knew she wouldn't reply, and she never did. She set Irie back on her feet and ax her to show us to the park where we might find her parents. Immediately, Irie took her by the hand and steam across the road. She never check for no vehicle, so once we reach the other pavement, I told her bout herself: if she was so comfort-able with strangers, then she should at least look after herself in other ways.

I try say it all softly as well. I took her by the hand and crouch down to her height, that's how you affi talk to naughty children, but she wouldn't look pon I. Her eye kept darting and she wouldn't stand still neither. She start chewing pon her blasted sleeve, and given the way it was already wet and threadbare, I could tell it was a habit. If her mama couldn't sew, I bet she spent a whole heap of money pon clothes.

'Something wrong with yuh?' I ax, and from the way she hung her head I could tell she was use to being chastise. 'This is for yuh own benefit, yuh know, yute?' Makeda told I-man to let her be, but there were things that Irie need fi overstand. I held Irie head between I hand, snap I finger and ax her if she was listening, but her eye glaze like one of the dunce yute inna the bottom set at school and she look right through I and went on chewing her blasted sleeve. 'Yuh can't run in the road, bredrin.'

'There weren't no car I looked,' she say, and boy, she hadn't said a lot past her name, but when she did speak, the words came out so fast you could hardly catch them. She never use no punctuation, no finger spaces, nothing. I figure she must've had something wrong with her. That's why nothing I said got through.

'Yuh nah look, I seen yuh,' I said, but she shake her head, telling me I hadn't seen what I definitely had. If I did carry on arguing with her she would've give I-man high blood pressure. Yutes love to go back and forth with you: 'Yes yuh did.' 'No I never'. 'Yes yuh did.' It was them favourite pastime. 'Fine, let's just go try find yuh parents them.'

I offer her I hand, but she went and took Makeda hand instead, as comfortable as anything, as if she'd known her

her whole life. I walk behind the pair of them, listening as Makeda ax her a whole load of question and as Irie answer them all rapid-fire. She was almost six, same as one of Makeda half-caste sister – so Makeda tell her. She live close by. She say never know what her parents did for work, but she knew them both have job, to which Makeda said good for them, but I knew a real brother would never let him woman work in such a wicked environment as England. She went to some primary school I'd never heard of, so I figure it must've been one of them for special yutes. Whenever Irie would answer one of Makeda question, I'd see her hand snake in her trouser pocket and quickly stuff something in her mouth. I couldn't tell what it was, some biscuit or water cracker or something. I imagine she thought neither of we notice as well, so I never call no attention to it. Sometimes you affi save evidence to use against yutes, so when you later challenge them and them protest them innocence, you have a whole heap of example to use against them. Irie did eat as fast as she talk, and I'd never heard anyone eat so loud. Again, I did want to say something because it was bad manners to eat on the street – specially so fast. I did want to have her empty her pocket pon the pavement, so I could brush them clean, but it wouldn't've look too good if we did rock up to the park and deliver her to her parents bawling with a whole lot of snot running down her face, specially not in front of the English.

It nah take we long to arrive at St Andrews Park. We found it full of nuff family, but we never see no brothers or sisters and no one wasn't stressing, so we just sat on a bench a likkle out

68

the way, where nobody couldn't see I&I, but I&I could keep an eye pon them. I never want no one calling the pigs again.

Makeda tuck Irie between her knee and stroke her birthmark with the back of her forefinger. 'Where yuh get this?' Irie seem glad to have it mention.

'I was born with it in the hospital it's what makes me different and when I'm at school my teacher said she liked it now everyone says they want one as well but you can't get one unless you're born with it like I am.' She reach into her pocket again and stuff her face. She was getting more brazen.

'What yuh have there?' Makeda say.

'Digestives,' Irie say, between mouthfuls, spitting crumbs. She shove one in Makeda face. 'You want some Makeda?'

'Yuh shouldn't talk with yuh mouth full,' I said, but them both ignore it. It was all very well wanting to be bredrins with the yutes you were responsible for, but if Makeda was desperate to play nice all the time, then it meant I did affi be the sensible one.

'Thank yuh, Irie,' Makeda say, breaking the biscuit. 'Yuh know, yuh birthmark sort of look like a man with a tam,' Makeda went on, between bites. 'Like him a sing or something. Yuh know what a tam is, Irie? The kind of hat what Rasta wear. Jabari a Rasta. Yuh know what Rastas are?'

'My daddy don't wear hats cos he don't have any hair on his head.'

'I always thought bald man should wear hats more than anyone else – it must get cold up there,' Makeda said, and she poke Irie stomach and the likkle girl giggle and went all shy.

We must've sat on that bench for a further fifteen minutes before I declare that we were better off looking for Irie parent ourself, but Makeda never agree. She say I was being impatient and insist Irie parent would come back to the place them last have her. She say I don't know how it was to parent cos I was an only child. Then Irie say she need fi go toilet, so we head off anyway. We thought bout knocking pon people door and axing whether we could use them bathroom, like how we use to do when we was yutes inna the Gardens. But that was never going to run in St Andrews, so we decide to distance ourself from the park and find an alley where she could go bout her business in peace.

We pass another few rows of welcome-home-Mummy-and-Daddy, sugar-paper house, until we come to a cul-de-sac with a row of garages at its end. The garages were abandon and empty of car, the doors were either gone or open, one had a pile of cardboard mattress and rotten quilt set aside, so Makeda took Irie to another. She tell I-man to wait pon the road, in case Irie parents went past, so I went and sat pon another St Andrews front wall, and that's when I saw two English people pointing at I-man from across the way: a man and a woman. I try fi ignore them, but the two a them were soon in the road and the man was apologising to a driver whose car him walk in front of. It wasn't a proper apology, though. I know cos him never even look at the driver. In fact, him never take him eye from I&I.

It wouldn't've seem like much to a bystander; them would've see the white couple ax a black boy a couple of question, seen the black boy respond, then watch the white couple leave. But with them arrival come the chance to do the right thing, the chance for a small revenge, a momentary victory: the very reason that I could've begin the story here and not with Angela. It wasn't as though I could've ignore it neither; it come right to where I was sat, stood in front of I face, chest swollen, breathless and self-important, in the shape of that very same white English couple, who I was bout to learn were call the Roskillys. I fed them lies, though them would never have known. And when Makeda and Irie come back from behind the garage, I quickly interrupt them idle conversation. 'Makeda, I affi tell yuh something *bad*,' I said, and I check over I&I shoulder, but the Roskillys were long gone. 'Irie can't hear neither.'

Makeda say: 'One sec, Jabari man, Irie telling me something.' But I swear I couldn't wait. I took ahold of Irie and crouch to her level, same way I had when telling her not to cross the road. I point to the garage them.

'Irie, I need yuh to go back over there and wait for I&I a minute. We're not going anywhere, I promise, I just need to borrow yuh bredrin from yuh, OK? Hear what, if yuh can stay over there a whole five minute then I'll buy yuh something nice to eat and yuh can keep it in yuh pocket, all right?' The likkle girl eye lit up. 'All right.' I watch as she did as she was told, waiting until she was outta earshot. 'We've been bredrins a while now, init, Makeda?' I still hadn't taken I&I attention from Irie, who arrive at the garage and was searching for something to busy herself with. 'Bout what now? Ten years? Longer? From when we born really, isn't it?'

'Something like that,' Makeda said. I could hear the mistrust, mistrust that never speak to the length of our friendship but rather to the separation of our respective allegiances – I could hear the Joyce in her.

'Yuh trust I-man, yes? Yuh know say I have I&I head set firmly atop I shoulder? Yuh know say I-man is not like the rest of them there yutes at the centre?'

'Just come out with it, Jabari man. Yuh scaring me with all this build-up, build-up. Yeah man, me trust yuh, yuh know say me trust yuh, yes.'

'OK,' I said, and I look pon her, her long eyelash them, her black iris. 'What kinda life yuh sibling have?'

'What?'

'What kinda life them have? Good or bad?'

'Why yuh a ax me that for, man? Them life all right. Enoch have a better job than him did when him was with my mama, so them better off.'

'What bout them spirit,' I said, and I touch I heart with I finger, then I touch I head. 'What bout them consciousness, them self-esteem?'

'Them half-caste and them live a South Bristol with them white mama,' Makeda said. The wind blew cold. She purse her lip and rub her arm. It made her more irritable. 'Them don't know nothing bout nothing, man, chuh. Them don't come down a St Pauls, not even for carnival.' She cut her eye after I. 'Better them don't come as well, cos if them come and bring Enoch, yuh papa would have unuh fling stone after him and my mama would try put a fish knife through him heart.'

'And whose fault is that?'

'Is what?'

'The fact them don't know themself?'

'Enoch fault.'

'Right, and who else?'

'Him woman, I guess.'

'Right!' I said, and I enthusiasm startle her so she hit I. 'Him woman have no business being the mother of black children,' I said. 'Yuh agree?'

'They're not black, them half-caste.'

I kiss I teeth. 'The yutes half-caste but the yutes black, man. Copper don't look pon them and think say cos them mama white them all right, him look pon them same way him look pon any redskin West Indian, him look pon them and see dog.'

Makeda cross her eyebrow and wave her hand in front of her face like a bad smell local. 'Jabari, I don't hate white people same way yuh hate them, yuh know? Them wicked, but yuh soon find everybody wicked; West Indian and Coolie, African, English, Chiney, Polish, the whole of mankind wicked, man. People them wicked Jabari, just like them bastard copper back there, and some people good still, but yuh can't tell the good from the wicked till them show yuh with them action.'

'But who is the worst, the very worst, Makeda? Who is at the top, no, the bottom, who is at the bottom?'

'White people,' Makeda admit, and then Irie wander back to us, so I spend another whole minute sending her away again.

I took a breath. 'Most black people spend them life doing

nothing against white people. Most of them won't lift a finger nor say not a cross word against them. Some a them even want be white: them tell them yutes not to marry nobody black dirt. The few black people that ever criticise them do it in them own home, them whisper them word of rebellion round a select few people who them feel, feel the same way, who them feel won't rat them out or use them words against them.' I move closer to her. 'Then yuh have a very few amount of black people who try make a change. Revenge, Makeda: the only way to restore balance. Jah create a balance world, a world that make perfect sense. Satan spawn white people, that's why the world fi them, because the world is Satan fi give. Only in Africa—'

'Jabari,' Makeda said.

Her attention kept travelling between Irie and I-man. I took ahold of her shoulder. 'No – listen, Makeda! Only in Africa can we be free: but before we leave for Africa we should make a difference to the here and now, right?'

Makeda screw up her face. 'Yuh papa don't agree. That's why him and Joyce don't see eye to eye. Levi don't care bout the people who want stay in England.'

'Him can't comprehend how unuh want languish here because Jah tell him to come from Jamaica and lead unuh to Ethiopia, that nah mean him nah care. Ras Levi care bout all black people.'

She shook herself free of I-man. 'If him care him wouldn't've kick Joyce out.'

'Him never kick her out: she left.'

'She left cos yuh papa don't care bout *all* black people.'

'Ras Levi would agree with everything I-man is saying.' I was near shouting now. We'd gone off-topic. Irie was looking over, concern. I force a smile and she smile back and return to her playing. I lower I voice again. 'Listen, not many opportunity arise where we can make a difference in this life, Makeda, but one come round just now, just now, when yuh take Irie round back of the garage.'

'What?'

'I just met Irie parent: cept them weren't her real parent.'

'Stop talking in riddles, man.'

'Two people walk up here; an English couple. Them cross the road over there and ax for I name, so I say, "What yuh axing for?" and them tell I that them lose fi them likkle girl. "So what?" I tell them, "If yuh accuse I-man of something then come out with the accusation," that's what I did say, because Jah know say I don't have no more patience to deal with no more devil today, but hear what them say: them say them daughter favour I-man, that them daughter a colour. So I say: "How do you mean she colour?" but I must've cut the woman off when she was talking because she get this attitude bout her. "I mean she *colour*," the woman say, and she say it just how you'd expect as well, like it was *I* accusing *her* of something. Yuh following, Makeda? Irie adopted, man. The white man and woman say them are the girl legal guardian.'

I seen as Makeda begin to overstand, as she begin to connect the same dot I had, because straightaway it had made a whole heap of sense; why Irie was the way she was. There was a home pon City Road, along between the bank and the

Cultural and Community Centre, and a lot of the yutes who live there went to special school.

'How yuh know say it's Irie them mean?' Makeda say, thinking.

'The man take out him wallet and show I one picture of the tree of them, then him take out some fancy pen and write him telephone number on the back.' I hand Makeda the photograph in question. 'Just now yuh admit that white people the worst, right?' Makeda look at it, Irie sat on the white woman knee, then she look down the alley toward Irie. She tore it in half and pocket the piece with a grimace. 'Yuh never see a white couple like this Makeda, them even too good fi come down a St Pauls fi the bank. I could tell the man was wealthy soon as him stride inna the road, like say car don't hit people no more. No wonder Irie do the same; they're teaching her how to be white, man.' I start gaining momentum. I could feel Makeda coming round, thinking with the same mind, reaching the same conclusion I had.

'I'll bet the council took Irie from her real mama just because,' I continue. 'The city never take no black yute from them mama with no good reason. We can already assume that Irie papa was never in the picture, this wouldn't have happen if she did come from a household with both her mummy and daddy, so we can assume that, right, right?' I said again, and Makeda nod – if reluctantly. 'Meaning Irie mama would affi work bout what, two, tree jobs just to make the rent money at the end of the month? That's assuming them even have a house or a room, assuming them don't stay with Irie nanny, but we can assume that, cos I reckon the council say that Irie was being left alone too long when her mama was there a work, but instead of fixing the problem and helping Irie mama, them add to her grief and teef her baby from her.' I pause to spit, I had a foul taste in I mouth; vexation and the salt from I-man earlier tears. 'Irie mama might've took her own life from the grief of it. City probably think it's better Irie with an English family anyway, them probably think them done the girl a favour.'

I glance over at Irie, imagining the life she live up until now. Makeda follow I eye. I knew she saw what I saw, but I did need her to be as angry as I was as well. 'We been looking for a West Indian couple this whole time, Makeda. Whole time in vain, but hear what: I'm not giving Irie to no white people, I'm taking her back to her real family.'

Makeda was very still. She never give her attention to Irie or I, her eye them drop and went glass again, travel somewhere into the future, or the past, I don't know. After a while she say: 'If we do that we'll be following right after yuh papa and Angela, going straight a prison.' She point her finger at I, her voice no longer faraway. 'I got things to do in this here life, yuh know Jabari, and if I go jail for this, every dream done, man. What yuh a talk bout have a name already, Jabari, it call kidnap.'

'I don't business bout what the English law say is wrong or right, Makeda. English law legalise slavery. It's not a kidnap, it's a rescuing.'

'Kidnapping exist everywhere—'

'Makeda!'

'What if them all right, though? Irie parent – not parent – yuh know what I mean, the white people; what if them all right?'

'What's all right when we a talk bout white people? An all-right white man don't what? Don't beat yuh up? Don't touch yuh? Don't spit inna yuh face and piss down yuh leg? An all-right white woman don't cry and phone a white man to run come save her? What's all right when we're talking bout white people? "All right." Yuh think all right can raise Irie?'

Makeda consider I-man. I could see her mind working fast, but time move slow. 'All right,' she say, after a minute. 'Joyce wouldn't want we fi just leave her here anyway and I'm not chasing after them.'

'Don't say all right unless it's all right, Makeda, unless yuh really down with what I-man a talk about, cos once yuh in this, yuh in this. No backing out.'

'Me know, man.'

'So yuh down, then?'

'Me already tell yuh yes, Jabari, man.' Again, she glance at Irie, who'd found a stick and look to investigate a small anthill. 'So what's the plan from here, then? Yuh want magic up Irie one perfect black family and wish her white parents forget her and adopt one next English baby and everybody live happily ever after?'

I blank her English humour. 'Plan is we'll take her some place to lay low a while, while her parents continue looking round here so. We'll take her back into St Pauls, maybe into Easton if we need, and then we find her real family. With that mark pon her face someone must recognise her, even if she hasn't been round since she was a baby, someone must.'

Above, there was a break in the grey cloud them and the sun land pon us. Makeda look fi Irie and shield her face. 'What happen when we find them?' she say, talking but not looking.

'Then them take her back – I don't know.'

Makeda eyelid narrow, face still averse. 'But what if them don't want her back?'

'What kinda family don't want them own pickney back?'

'My papa don't want me.'

'True.' I thought for a second. 'All right, well if them don't want her then maybe when Ras Levi come home, him can see to placing her inna next family, a black family.'

She face I-man once more. 'How?'

'I don't know.'

'We don't know when him will be out, neither.'

'He'll be out inna couple day, man. Them don't have nothing fi charge him with. And him will help I&I if I&I cannot sort it out ourself.'

'Disturbing the peace, being a threat to the community, loitering, drug-selling, them can charge him with whatever them want.' She count the possible charge pon her finger. 'And it's not like him can influence the city. City decide what yute go with what family and if them already decide Irie is with the white people them nah go change them mind because Ras Levi from St Pauls say so.'

'We'll work it out, man, Makeda. Right now, we just need

to do this. Every day Babylon get we down, every day them come inna St Pauls and violate we. Earlier, I overhear Miss Cornwall and that jankrow Battersby talking bout bowing down, not fighting back, learning to live and let live and them things there. I can't live like them, Makeda. I can't roll over backwards. It's not how I was raise. With this, we might be able to change that likkle girl life forever, yuh overstand?' I try another angle. 'Remember yuh sister what's Irie age, imagine it was one of yuh likkle siblings them who we found: imagine that.'

'Them have a white mother anyway.'

'But them daddy black. Enoch may be a coon, but him black still. At least them white mama choose to lie down with a bredda to make a baby. At least she did that.'

'All right,' Makeda said, and she exhale and look back to the sky as the grey did cloud the sun again, but this time I did believe her. 'All right.'

6

Years ago, the allotments were given to the St Pauls people as a means of appeasement, and, for once, RastafarI did accept the liarsment initiative so that we might grow our own ital food and live without eating them process rubbish. The lung a the inner city. Halfway between St Andrews and St Pauls, on a steep hill bound by Stony Lane and the railway line. A number of Rastas had plot, including Ras Levi, who never tend it, not because of negligence: Mr Mitchell, the site manager, would've strip we of the land otherwise. It was because him don't have the time, and so the task had fallen to I-man. The allotments soil was clay. You did affi keep the main path that border the plots a certain width, and you couldn't chop into the banks to expand your plot. You affi prevent weed and seeding spreading, and bonfire was only allow between November and March. Some people did keep chicken and rabbit and bee. Some people dug pond, others fill old bathtub with water and built ramp for amphibian to come and go. Irie, happy in her ignorance, point at them all and identify whatever she could put a name to. The things she nah recognise, she try to pocket, and she strop when I never let her.

Each April and August, Mr Mitchell would come round with him pork pie and wellington boot and make a note of the unkept plot, and soon you'd see them given to somebody new, and there was a whole queue of people waiting for even the smallest piece of land. Mr Mitchell said you couldn't bring old carpets onto the plot, and you certainly couldn't fit to live in your shed, but Ras Levi told I to ignore that particular regulation. Him respect Mr Mitchell, who was a hermit of a man, well knowledgeable bout the earth, but Ras Levi want the shed ready for all manner of calamity, so we kept it stock with bokkle water and tin pulse, enough to live on for a couple days. A while back I'd found a rug roll inna skip on City Road, so I took it, brush it, and staple it down. I'd also built a low bed frame and lain a single mattress which took up most of the floor space. There were a couple shelf holding small books and plant pot, some ganja.

We saw Mr Mitchell nursing his plot as we arrive. Him call hello and tell we fi mind that it had twice rain since I'd last been. I thank him and we beeline for the shed, wanting Irie outta sight as quickly as possible. I unlock it with the key I always kept on I person, making sure, as I always do, that Mr Mitchell couldn't catch sight of the illegal trappings inside. I lock back the door and we made ourself comfortable – ready to pass the time. Makeda ax why we had the shed set up like so, with all the comfort and the secrecy, so I told her bout Ras Levi paranoia, and despite the reflective mood that had taken her spirit since leaving St Andrews, she laugh after we. 'Unuh no better than the mad people who prepare for the next coming of Christ,' she say. 'Yuh soon go door to door preaching bout the end of days.'

'Shut up, man: yuh too bright.' I hand them both a bokkle of water from where them was kept overneath the pallet bed, and an apple and banana each, and ax why Irie hadn't thought to tell I&I that she was adopted.

'I don't know,' Irie said, accepting the gifts gratefully. She put aside the water and start pon the apple, biting into it like a jenny might.

'Well then tell I&I something yuh do know,' I said.

'Where yuh real parents from?' Makeda ax. 'Them West Indian or African?'

'It's the same thing,' I mutter, but Makeda only told I not to confuse things.

'West Indian, my mummy's colour's the same as me,' Irie said.

'What bout yuh daddy?' Makeda say.

'Don't say colour,' I said, at the same time.

'She say colour, not coloured,' Makeda say, but still I carry on.

'Black is not a dirty word, yuh shouldn't avoid it. Which part a Jamaica yuh mama come from? Yuh *black* mama.'

'She never say she was Jamaican,' Makeda say, 'she could be a Trini or a Bajan, or even a Kittian. What's yuh mummy surname?'

I frown. 'If we went by her surname we might think she was Scottish.'

83

'My mummy told me she's from Jamaica,' Irie said. She had her knee tuck up to her chest. 'I don't know from what part.'

Makeda smile. We were making progress. 'If we name the parish yuh wouldn't recognise it, no?'

Irie shake her head.

'Yuh know where she live now?' I ax.

She shake her head again.

'Was she born a Jamaica?' Makeda ax, and she leant forward to wipe apple spittle from the edge of the girl mouth.

Irie held her face still. 'I . . . I don't know.'

'It's OK, baby.' Makeda say. 'We're axing yuh a whole lot of question, yuh don't affi know them all: nobody know everything.'

'Yuh know St Pauls or Easton very well?' I ax.

She shake her head.

Makeda turn to I&I. 'I think we should take her to the Mother, yuh know, see if Joyce recognise her.'

I almost laugh. 'No chance.'

'What's the Mother?' Irie said.

Makeda never skip a beat. 'Joyce whole set-up fi sisters, Jabari. Her whole life work: plus she know everybody who need knowing – Joyce the best person to ax, man.'

'No, if we need help then we'll wait for Ras Levi. I-man can't involve Joyce.'

'Yuh papa there in jail, Jabari. If this is going to be done, it needs doing now.'

There was a knock pon the shed door.

Makeda neck snap toward I. She was rarely nothing other

than cool, so I heart start to beat double time too. 'Jabari,' she whisper. I motion for her to keep ahold of Irie and keep her quiet. The walls were paper thin – the smallest of movements could be heard from outside. There was no way it was the beastman; even if the Roskillys call the copper straightaway them would've gone to meet them at them yard, or them would've search St Andrews Park, them would never have known to check the allotments.

'Mr Mitchell?' I call.

'It's Prince,' said the voice, and I nearly groan aloud. Prince was Friday boy, and never had a name been at greater odds with its bearer.

'What yuh want, man?'

'To come in?'

'Let him in,' Makeda said, still whispering.

'What?'

'It's not the coppers. Let him in.'

'We can't trust him,' I said. 'I go school with him, Makeda, we can't trust him. Yuh never know what him a go say or do. Him a go take one look at Irie and snitch, if not to the copper, then him will run him mouth to everybody inna St Pauls.'

'Yuh never even go a school, Jabari.'

'I still know how him stay.'

'Him will get suspicious if we send him away.'

'Him never even know say yuh here.'

'I do actually,' Prince call from outside. 'I can hear everything the two of you are saying. I know Makeda's in there with you. That's why I'm here, actually. I saw you come in here with a little girl when I was passing on the school bus. I asked the driver if he could stop . . . so, are you gonna let me in or not?'

Makeda tip her head to the side, sending I to the door. Everything in I-man was telling I to keep the man outside, but I let him in same way.

If Friday was foremost amongst the Day-by-Days, then Prince was heir to him throne. Him fancy himself as something of a sweet-boy. Him keep a whole box of toothpick in him pocket and one in him mouth – you could hear him pocket rattle when him jog up the school stairs. Him was slender and shortish and black like shiny shoe, and since him was known for having a nice voice, him sing ska to the girls in St Pauls. Prince never sing no real reggae though, him only had an interest in two-tone and fusion and them kinda thing there. Him like the reggae what the English yutes like. And when him weren't singing, Prince show the brothers one personality, and the sistrens another. Him never have a thing call shame. Him whistle and catcall after Lady Luck, and inna place full up of West Indian in love with the thought of Africa, him was known for telling the pretty girls that him could take them to the Motherland. It was said that him still have family inna Accra, and Kumasi, and Cape Coast. There was even a rumour that him was of distant relation to Nkrumah. I open the shed door to the rumour source: Prince was lean up against the side, loyal pick in him mouth. Him take it out when the door fully open and I bolt it behind him.

'How's everybody doing this afternoon?' him say with a smile, and with the four of us inside, the place was well cramp.

Him remove him sunglasses from him face, fold them and hang them from him collar. Irie shuffle further back on the bed, until her back was against the wall. I was force to stand and Prince manage fi find space beside Makeda. Irie still hadn't finish her apple. She eat fast but her bites were small, and she avoid the core so much so that there was still nuff flesh between her mouth and the fruit miggle when she drop it in her lap and left it there. 'It's nice in here, eh,' said Prince, 'you wouldn't think it from the outside.'

I had reason to mistrust him. I may not have attended Greenway very often, but I had it on good authority that him was spot in the teacher lounge. I wouldn't have put it past him neither, him was like all Day-by-Days: a man out for himself. I'd never had much to do with him in the short time him had been in St Pauls. We'd never exchange more than a word in passing, but it was more than possible that him was as untrustworthy as him daddy, so I plan to keep the truth of Irie a secret. I try to communicate that to Makeda, try to remind her of her promise to keep I bawling a secret too, but she stubbornly refuse fi look pon I. Instead, she let him eeks himself up next to her. And him never have no broad shoulder or nothing neither, so him get real close – the two of them thigh a touch, and for a second I thought him was bout to put him arm round her like say she was him woman. 'Friday told me about what happened with Angela. You all right?' him say.

'Yeah man,' Makeda said. 'Yuh can't help these things, isn't it?'

'Still a shame,' him say. 'You gonna tell me who this is then?'

Prince smile at Irie. Him did think him have a winning smile. You could tell. Him teeth were bright white though – I affi admit. 'This nice girl you're trying to keep from me. What's your name, little one?'

'Why've you got that in your mouth?' Irie ax, pointing at his toothpick.

'Something to chew on, take your mind off things, eh. You want one?' Him pull him packet of one hundred from him pocket. Irie shook her head. It was a bit quiet after that, Prince broke it with a hum. Him did want we to believe him comfortable, despite the awkwardness of his being there. Him was a lot of things, but not a dunce; him know say him was an outsider. I never know the song him a hum neither, but that was all part of him game. Him did want one of we fi ax him. Then him would've said something like *you wouldn't know it, it's a rare groove*, and I would've had to box him in the mouth.

'Why yuh here, Prince?' I ax. 'What yuh want with Makeda?'

'Only to pass on my sympathies and to hear what happened this morning from the lady herself.' Him smirk, and it stay on him face like plastic. 'But now I want to know what you were worried I'd tell the coppers bout? Is it anything to do with what happened earlier?'

I look at Makeda, and she at I. 'It wasn't nothing, man.'

Prince stood up, 'It didn't sound like nothing.' A thought cross him mind. 'Irie isn't Angela's child, is she? No, Angela don't have any.' Him frown. 'Whose is she?'

'I cousin,' I said, at the same time as Makeda insist she was her neighbour. Prince smirk widen inna a grin. I know say him did think say him was the smartest in whatever room him was in. Him was a real, blasted pain.

'So are you going to tell me what's going on, or am I going to run and tell the whole of St Pauls?' him say. 'A little information can be more dangerous than a lot, you know?'

'Fine, we'll tell yuh' Makeda said, 'But yuh affi swear to keep yuh mouth shut.'

'Makeda!' I said. 'Yuh can't tell him nothing more, man. Yuh already let him inside.'

'Yuh hear him, Jabari. If we don't tell him then him will run tell everybody and anybody that him see us going inna the allotment together with a likkle girl, soon as the white people go to the police, which them will, if them haven't already, them will come a St Pauls and someone will point straight at us. Think, man.'

'The people them won't talk to no police,' I say.

'Don't count on it,' Prince say. Him would never have been so smug if I did bust him lip, but I held back and listen as Makeda explain who Irie was. At first Prince smirk stay where it was, but it falter as Makeda went on, and by time she finish him face was solemn.

'You guys need to take her back.' Him stand up, as if him was about fi go somewhere, so I took a step toward him. Behind Prince, I saw Irie pull her knee even closer to her chest, as she press herself into the corner and try to shrink as far from the confrontation as she could.

'It's too late to leave. Yuh better sit down, yuh know, rudeboy,' I said, and Prince eye I, before him took back him seat. I told Irie everything was bless, but I could see she never believe I-man. Some yutes were like that though; if you ever show them any aggression then them won't never trust you again; some yutes were soft like that.

'You know what you've done is illegal?' Prince go on. 'It don't matter how you dress it up. It's kidnap.'

Makeda look at I-man. 'What me tell yuh?' she say.

'It's not kidnap, it's a rescuing.'

'Say that in the dock,' Prince said, without humour. 'Soon as you go back to St Pauls the police will arrest both of you.' Him stretch back pon the bed again, propping himself up, as if him felt him were in control once more, and him outstretch leg almost kick I shin.

'The coppers don't even know yet,' I say.

'How'd you know? First thing I'd do is call the police if my baby went missing.'

'Yeah, cos yuh a bloodclart snitch. Even if them have call the police it's not like every police is gonna get the alert at the same time: far as them concern it's just a missing child, children go missing all the time. This one a missing black child as well.'

'Yuh affi promise yuh won't say nothing, Prince,' Makeda said.

Him meet her eye. 'If you found her in St Andrews then her parents are rich. I bet you anything her real family is poor – far as I'm concerned she hit the jackpot. She'll live in a big house for the rest of her life, eat the best of food, have a full belly, and they'll put her into the best schools as well: she'll be set up for life.'

'So?' I said. 'She won't see no black people at home, in her neighbourhood, in her school. She'll grow up surround by English people her whole life, not knowing her own.'

'You shouldn't underestimate what education can do. Anyway, if their name's Roskilly, they're not English, they're Cornish.' And him did give out a big yawn when him say that.

'How yuh know that?' Makeda said. Prince shrug and fiddle with him pick.

'So what them Cornish? Don't matter if them Spanish,' I said.

'So they're a different tribe.'

'English people don't have no different tribe.'

'Yeah they do, just like my dad's Twi and my mum's Ga. Why d'you think they're fighting the IRA? It's just tribalism. Cornish people are the same as Irish. If it came to a war Cornwall would fight on Ireland's side. Read a book.'

'*I* might fight on Ireland side,' Makeda said. She was trying to keep the peace. She wasn't afraid of confrontation like Irie was, clearly, but she also couldn't be bother to separate a scrap. You could hear how likkle she could be bother in her voice. She want to move on, but as usual, I was going to say what I want to.

'I ain't fighting on no white man side,' I said. 'Them all racist, even the Irish. We was put on English people sign next to them, next to dog as well, but that never stop no dog from biting I&I, same way it don't make Irish people any less racist. I might like them more than I like the English, but I like them from a distance, iyah. It don't change nothing bout how I feel toward white people as a whole.'

91

Prince screw up him face. 'They can't all be racist – that don't even make sense! How can you know how everybody feels? Have you met every white person in the whole world? You ever been to Yugoslavia?'

'Don't matter if I haven't met all of them. History prove I&I right. How wouldn't them man be racist inna Yugoslavia, yuh tell I-man that, since yuh feel say yuh know everything? How would them white people over there a Yugoslavia avoid the same disease what catch every other white person in the world? I don't want Irie round none of them.'

'Lucky for her you don't have no say in the matter, eh. You're not her parent. You say you want to take her home as well. Do you even know who her family is?'

'That's what we need to work out,' Makeda say, as she reach behind her and stroke Irie leg. Irie let her too, which I suppose made sense; it was Prince and I she was nervous round.

'So you don't even know if the city took them with good reason?' Prince said, and him sit up all dramatic. 'Her parents could be dead. Could be in prison! Could've gone back to wherever they're from.'

'Like I said, them never have a good reason man,' I said. I was vex now. Partly, I want to cool off so Irie could relax again, but I couldn't with a coconut Day-by-Day talking as if him knew everything. 'What's a good reason to teef somebody yute? If it was a good reason, like her parents dead, then her uncle or her aunty or her nanny would've taken her in. This is why it never make no sense. What black people yuh know would want them family to go inna the system? I know plenty of people in the Gardens who've had them yutes took from them, and the reason is never any good.'

'I don't know – there's a lot of people who shouldn't've had kids and there's a lot of people who don't want the ones they do have,' Prince said, and I saw Makeda give him a look like she was all sorry for him, but I nah business what him was on about, so I turn and ax Irie if she knew why the council had taken her away from her mama, but she only knew that she'd been with her white family since she was tree years old.

'Don't you think it's strange that she went off with you guys in the first place?' Prince said, continuing the age-old tradition of talking bout yutes in front of them as if them weren't there. Irie never seem to mind, though. She was less edgy, content being with Makeda.

'It's not strange,' I said. 'It would be strange if she want to stay with her fake, white parents.'

'No it wouldn't. That's not how babies work,' Prince say.

Makeda purse her lips and tilt her head, rejoining the conversation. 'Angela tell me nuff yutes inna the system nah have no real sense of danger, that them try friend everyone cos them don't have no one, yuh know?'

'See it there,' I said triumphantly.

Prince never respond. Him look directly at Irie. 'Irie, what do you want to do, eh? Have these two asked you that?'

'True,' Makeda said. 'Irie, what yuh want? Yuh wanna go back to the Roskillys in St Andrews or yuh want stay with we and try find yuh mama?'

'Yuh can't ax her that,' I scoff. 'She don't know what's best for her.'

We all look to Irie, who had bitten back into the apple and had more fruit on her face. Makeda reach to lend another hand, but this time Irie push her aside and wipe the apple crumb with her own palm. 'I want to stay with you, Makeda,' she said, suddenly bright-eye and licking her hand, happy to be involve, and happy to please.

'Then it's sekkle then.' Makeda drew Irie onto her lap, assuring her that she'd made the right choice. 'Unuh can drop it, now.'

'Fine, then it's settled,' Prince said, and him lean back pon him elbow.

'Yuh better not say nothing,' I said threateningly.

Prince lift him head and met I&I eye. 'You know,' him say, and him went on speaking to Makeda without taking him attention from I, 'Friday might know whose baby she is.' And him ignore Irie insistence that she wasn't a baby.

'How would him know Irie?' I said. 'Unuh just get here yesterday.'

'It's true though, come like Friday know everybody,' said Makeda. 'Him might've heard bout a yute with a birthmark like that.' She point at it. 'I don't know, might know something. We don't have much of a choice anyway, since you don't want bring her to the Mother.' She turn to Prince. 'We'll take her to yours first.'

Soon as we was back in St Pauls I had everybody and them mama come up to I and give them condolence and ax after Ras Levi, like say him had pass on to the next. How them expect

I-man to know how him fare? I had as much of a clue as them.
Still, I told them that him was doing just fine, and them nod
and tell I-man not to worry cos him was strong – but I knew
him was strong, them needn't've said nothing. There were
still nuff copper about, lurking in them riot gear, but them
nah think nothing of Irie, who was taking turn pon each of
our shoulder.

  We made it to the Gardens, where there weren't no pigs,
and an elder tell I that the Rastas them had call one meeting
over at Miss Nefertari house. A few yutes come up to we and
ax who Irie was, and I did affi smack a yute ear who guess that
Irie was Makeda daughter, but Makeda only laugh and Prince
mutter something I never catch. We bump into the rudeboys
and sticksmen who were sat atop the Allegro bonnet next to a
boombox that was playing Junior Murvin 'Police and Thieves'.
Them tip them hat to Makeda for throwing the brick at the
beastman and told her to pass them salutations to Joyce. Them
love use word like *salutations*, it make them feel over smart,
even though most of them spent them short school life in the
dunce class before being expel. Them apologise for not being
able to stop the pigs. Then one of them, a fresh-face redskin
boy, push to the front of the group. 'Yo, Makeda,' him say, and
you could tell by the way him walk that him did think say him
was hot stuff. 'Yuh hear the coppers kill Angela?'

  'What?' Makeda say, at the same time as Prince and I. 'Nah,
that's rubbish man.' I'd never seen her so adamant. 'I would've
heard.'

  'Yuh hearing it now,' the rudeboy said.

'It's just a rumour,' another one went.

'It's true man,' insist the redskin yute. 'If them never kill her then them beat her half dead.'

'Angela can handle herself,' Makeda say, and I could tell she want to box him. Then the rudeboy took a revolver outta him jacket pocket. It was snub nose and dirty, and look as though him might've made it himself. I felt Prince stiffen beside I-man and Makeda fell quiet. 'We can handle ourself if them come back too,' him say, before telling we fi find him if any more trouble start. Him return to the back of the group and Makeda never speak for the rest of the conversation. The other rudeboys did give Irie some cash and let her try on them gold chain, but them say them nah know whose yute she was. Them never show much interest in Irie, anyway. All them want fi know was whether we were gonna pay Ras Levi way outta jail with the pardna money, or whether we was gonna start a commotion them could join.

'Yuh only wanna know bout the money so unuh can teef it,' I said warily, keeping an eye on the redskin yute. Against the strange backdrop of them laughter and Murvin falsetto, the gun in him pocket was made all the more threatening. Thankfully, Prince spot Friday walking the gangway that led to him and Prince home. Him had him arm slung round some blonde English prostitute who was at least two heads taller than him. Prince call him over, so we excuse ourself from the rudeboys' company.

Makeda came close to I ear. 'Them mad,' she say.

I nod. 'Same time I get it, though, yuh know?'

'Yeah, me get it as well, but . . . I don't know, yuh can't kill coppers. And there's no way Angela dead. Mash up probably, but not dead. Joyce would've send someone to come find me. I'm sure.'

'Mmmh,' I say in return, as Friday approach. The man was as dark as him only child, with a voice like honey, and him reputation did precede him: him was known for picking em up and laying em down. Him did keep him hand pon him woman backside as him stroll over. Him woman was the kind who would've been outside a different lock-in every weekend – no doubt where she would've met Friday.

True to him word, all those years ago, I'd only ever seen Friday with English woman, Polish at a stretch. Him was the kind of man who said him couldn't get down with sisters cos them did remind him of him mama. The kind of man who said black woman have too much sass. I-man knew plenty of guys in school who said the same: it was a Day-by-Day favourite. Personally, no milk-skin Delilah could ever tempt I-man. The transparency of them complexion would freak I-man out. I figure them must glow in the dark when them did take off fi them clothes, the blood in them blue and green vein like lava lamps in the night. Friday arrive at the head of our ragtag group, and him woman try fi slow him petting, but still him persist. It took a different kind of man to make a hooker prudish. 'Friday,' the blonde say, swatting at him arm. 'Friday!'

'Hush, woman.' Him claw at her bottom with him ring finger.

'Friday!' She laugh as him left her behind and began at her

97

ear and neck. I set Irie down and let her run toward the local yutes who were busy driving the abandon family car – she shouldn't affi see such things, it weren't righteous.

'How was school?' Friday said, without raising him head from the woman neck.

'It was good,' Prince said, and him split him pick between him molar and toss the two pieces. I study him for a sign that him fada antic bother him, and found several in the twitching of him mouth and him refusal to raise him head – in fact, neither fada or son look directly at the other; them give them attention to the floor, passers-by; them lick the tip of them finger and felt the wind; them did do anything but look pon one another, and it seem them did do so without realising, too.

'And whose baby is that, Jabari?' Friday said. 'Levi got you starting young eh.'

'She not Jabari yute,' Makeda said.

'Oh, then is she yours?' Finally, him lips left the woman. Him held him arm round her waist and face we. Makeda grit her teeth. And I imagine the man only name him son Prince to crown himself king.

'I'm sorry to hear bout your old man,' the woman said to I-man. I nod in thanks.

'Yes, it is a real shame.' Friday smooth him chin. 'A real shame what they did to you as well, eh.' Him touch I bruise cheek with him knuckle. 'Why haven't you cleaned yourself yet? You should have done it straightaway, it's not good to let them see you down and out, eh. Not that you should have been in St Pauls at that time, anyway. You should have been in school with Prince. Has anyone told you that? I bet your mama did. If not then she certainly should have, eh.' Him did speak with such familiarity you would've thought we was big bredrins. I nudge Prince, whose attention had wander back to the rudeboys and sticksmen, prompting him to refocus the conversation.

'So you don't recognise the girl then, Papa?' Prince said, scratching a mark from him blue jeans, and this time him went to meet him papa eye, albeit hesitantly, but by then Friday had return to kissing him woman, and I did watch as what likkle piece of light Prince had left in him face disappear.

'No, I do not, but I tell you what, Prince.' Friday dug inna him pocket and hand him only child some silver coin. 'Fetch your dinner from Mrs Hutchinson and stay out until after dark.' Him set him own attention on the rudeboys with a grimace. 'And stay away from those idiot boys, eh.' Him turn to him woman. 'You got any money in your purse?' The hooker hand Prince a pound note and the pair left without saying goodbye.

'I'm not exactly an expert, but don't *him* affi pay *her*?' Makeda said. 'Why she giving yuh money for?'

'He's not paying,' Prince tell we quietly. 'They're friends.'

'Friends,' I said sarcastically, but instantly I felt a twinge of regret.

'Yeah,' him say. We watch as the pair climb the stairs and unlock the door to one of the upstairs maisonette. Prince scan the Gardens; there were only a few people who'd notice the affair: the rudeboys were laughing, and the expressions of two elders sat outside an open-doored house playing Charley

Pride made them disapproval known. Prince pluck another toothpick from him box and twist it between him back teeth. Makeda never say a word.

'Yeah, your pops is off, iyah,' I said, trying to offer something of a comforting sentiment, but it was obvious Prince want nothing more than to change the subject. And when Irie return from the playground she did give him that opportunity.

'How'd you like the Gardens, Miss Irie?' Prince said, injecting life into him voice.

'I met that girl.' Irie point at the child in question, a cute likkle something with her hair inna pineapple. Miss Reynolds grandbaby. 'And her mum said I could go over and play so can I go over to her house, Makeda?'

'Where yuh please there?' I said.

'Please.'

'Not today,' Makeda say, embracing her motherly duty and stroking the likkle girl head. I said how good it was seeing her so tender, and she box I arm to prove she wasn't going soft.

'You in school tomorrow, Makeda?' Prince said. 'We could get the bus back together?'

'Nah,' Makeda said, making an apologetic face. 'Me and Jabari need to figure out what we're doing with Irie, init. Yuh gonna be all right tonight?'

Prince bridle and straighten him back. 'Yeah, I'll be fine.'

'Yuh can come to the café if you want?'

'Yeah, yeah. Maybe, I'll come by later.' Then him stare out across the Gardens. 'Later, Jabari. See you in a bit, Miss Irie.'

'Later,' I said, and Irie wave after him as him did head

deeper inna the Gardens with him hand in him trouser pocket. 'Yo, Prince,' I call and him turn. 'There's a meeting going on at Miss Nefertari house, there'll be food, yuh want something to eat?'

Him shake him head. 'I'll be all right.'

I return Irie to I&I shoulder and we took our leave. Once outta the estate we did stop at the pavement edge, the Mother one way, Miss Nefertari yard another. 'Him gone be all right?'

'Probably,' Makeda said, looking back in him direction. 'I think this happens a lot.' I nod. 'Yo, yuh reckon we could use some of the money from the pardna to find Irie somewhere to live?' Makeda say. 'Not a lot, obviously. I don't think it would take much. We could give the money to Joyce, have her find Irie a family in London or the Midlands or something, somewhere out the way. It's a reach, but what do yuh reckon, if worse comes to worst?'

'What, yuh fully on board now?'

'When I say something, I mean it, Jabari.'

'I don't know,' I said. 'That's why I want to wait for Ras Levi to come home, so I could ax him bout using the pardna, yuh know?' I told Makeda that I'd take Irie to mine. I figure since all the Rastas were there, someone was bound to recognise her, and if not then I promise I'd bring her to the Mother Earth in the morning.

'Look at yuh.' She smile. 'A stubborn yute like yuh a compromise fi me? Keep it up and I might get the wrong idea, Jabari, start wondering how yuh really feel bout me.' I went to insist that she shouldn't be getting any ideas at all, that there was nothing to get ideas bout, when she reach up and kiss I cheek like she had that morning, but this time she stay there a bit longer. It was more sudden. Urgent, maybe. The reason wasn't as clear or as safe as a greeting. 'Me know me nah say nothing before, but I'm glad yuh was with me earlier, Jabari,' she say, her voice deep and low. 'It's hard to go through them things alone, yuh know? It mess with yuh either way, of course, but specially when yuh alone.' She half-smile and turn to leave before I could tell her I felt the same. A few stride away she turn and wave with both hand, blowing Irie kisses. She left before I could tell her that I'd never let anyone disrespect her ever again . . . but inna way, I was glad she went when she did, because I hadn't even put words to the promise and still them felt so hollow.

7

There weren't enough Rastas in St Pauls to split into commune of Twelve Tribe or Bobo Shanti: some of we believe RastafarI was a religion, some say it was a way of life – a spirituality that never require the bondage of definition. Some were lead singers in touring band (though not the kind Prince idolise), others did play and listen only to the beating drum. Some, like Ras Levi, read and study the King James simply because His Imperial Majesty upheld it as the word of God; others claim it was a tool use to hurt our people and was doctor to remove the African empress, Sheba – among other things. Each man was Negus of him own household, and inside him own four wall him practise whatever him feel was right, but within the walls of the Cultural and Community Centre, and in the public eye, we were of one spirit, mind and body: a united front stood against the sheep masses, so some of the ganja-smoking man who did roost pon and round the wall bounding Miss Nefertari yard wore them locs in colourful headwrap of reds and yellows, and others never.

'Your hair's long like a girl's, Jabari,' Irie said, running her hand along I&I loc, picking them up and trying to tress them. 'Your hair's longer than mine and it goes down but mine goes up when you comb it out does it stay up or go down?'

'I haven't done nothing much to it since I-man was a child, yuh know, Irie. It only goes down cos it's loc. Yuh should loc yuh hair as well, yuh know, it would suit yuh.'

'Maybe,' she say, and I swear if you listen closely you could hear a yute think. 'I dunno.'

'Yuh ever read the Bible?'

'When I go to Sunday School, I read the Bible.'

'Yuh know Samson, who was with Delilah, and the building him bring down when everybody a eat and drink inside? Yuh know Samson hair was longer than I hair but it was the same style? I papa hair is loc as well, yuh know Irie, but Ras Levi hair is the same length as Samson hair. I wish yuh could've met him, yuh know, but him away right now.' She ax where him there, but I never answer her.

The Ras greet we as we arrive and tell I the rest of the Idrin them were inna the kitchen, discussing what action fi take against Babylon. I could hear the drum sound from inside as well, so I knew somebody was playing. That, along with the bass in the man voice, must've scare Irie bad, cos she put her sleeve in her mouth and shut up. I figure it would've been the first time Irie had been round so many black people since the city steal her. It must've been a surprise, but I figure once she get over the shock of it, it would be a welcome one. To be honest, I couldn't say, cos it wasn't something I much relate to: I did spend so much time in St Pauls that sometime I forgot what the rest of the country look like. The coppers them try remind I as often as them could, but without them it might've felt like I was in Ethiopia already.

Miss Nefertari yard was often the best example of that.

If reasonings weren't held in the Cultural and Community Centre then them went on in I&I yard, and that is when Miss Nefertari would best perform the role given her by Ras Levi. She would assemble the cooks and the bakers, borrow next table from one neighbour and lay them with our best china-ware – the ones with the gold-effect rim and rib edge. She usually kept them inna cabinet inna the front room. It had its own lock and key and a crochet dolly sat up pon its head. Miss Nefertari had various ornament and things dot throughout the yard: felt-shade lamp; stuff animal and knit dolly; a drink trolley where we did keep a jug full of water next to a bowl of hard-boil sweetie, though sometimes the jug was fill with Ras Levi carrot juice – him one contribution inna the kitchen. All round the yard were artificial flowers, bookshelf full up of Ras Levi Bible: the walls were cover with black felt scroll with gold emboss outline of the islands inna the Caribbean sea; religious plaque; a painting of a loc Christ with a crown of thorns and another painting of the same loc Christ sat at the Last Supper. With all that cram inside Miss Nefertari yard, you would've thought it impossible to fit every Ras in St Pauls inside, specially given them were confine to downstairs (Miss Nefertari wouldn't allow anyone up inna the bedroom them), but somehow, we did manage.

Forwarding inside, I step on so many toe I get sick of

apologising, bredda. Every seat in the yard was took, and from the kitchen I could hear the brothers them chant RastafarI whenever Jah name was invoke. When the sistrens did notice Irie, them come up from all round, stroking her face and squeezing her hand, and Irie find her voice again, and every time them come she did lean forward to hug them and want fi be in them arm – if only for a second. Them call her precious and did ax whose baby she was. I told them I never know, that I'd found her wandering the St Pauls streets, which got everyone worry and them parcel her round the room, but to no avail – no one nah recognise her. When all of the younger woman were flummox, like a big bag of rice, them deposit her on the dining table, where tree elder woman was sat, them hand resting atop them cane. Immediately, Irie look for I in the room full of new face, so I push through the people only to stand and hold her hand, and after that she was content to eat the hot piece of festival she was pass and to consider the three old woman who were patiently considering her.

I sent a pray skyward, because if them never recognise her, no Rasta would. The tree woman were encyclopaedia – ax them one thing bout St Pauls and them will tell you ten, even Ras Levi would seek them wisdom out. Them rub them chin, tap them cane, them headscarf fix firmly atop them high head and them eyelid sag over them eye like slow raindrop what refuse fi fall. Them were woman who name would never know because no one ever refer to them by any given name. Them were only call *mama*, and them only call one another *sister*. The room turn quiet fi hear them conversation, but it was of likkle use: most of the room could only catch the odd word. The woman spoke a raw, countrify version of Patois, and when combine with an intonation of them own design, born of a lifelong and insular friendship, it was near impenetrable, but you could get by if you open your ears and follow them mouth.

Elder One: Hmm, I don't know her face, sister. Either a unuh see her family in her face?

Elder Two: She look like one of Nancy granddaughter.

Elder Tree: Nancy nah have no grandchildren.

Elder Two: Nancy have bout tree a them, sister.

Elder One: Nancy have bout tree a them, true, but this one can't be one a Nancy – Nancy don't let her grandbaby outta her sight. Nancy too strict.

Elder Two: Nancy keep her affair in order, a true.

Elder Tree: What bout Maxine, she have a whole heap a yute.

Elder Two: What, Maxine down Denbigh Street?

Elder One: No, Maxine with the bad back, Maxine?

Elder Tree: Yes, with the bad back Maxine; she have a whole heap a babyfather, and a whole heap of yute too, and now her baby have babyfather and them have yute as well.

Elder One: She must be a great-great-grandmother by now.

Elder Tree: She must, yes.

Elder Two: Yuh would never think yuh could get a bad back from laying down.

The woman laugh.

Elder Two: Maxine full a dysfunction, man.

Elder One: The baby not Maxine family, yuh would've seen it in her small nose. This baby nose don't small like so, see the nostril broad like I&I nose.

Elder Two: Yes, sister. It's the nose. How it shape like so. Yes, yuh right.

Elder One: What bout Cornwall, she have a lot of pickney? Couple of them must have baby by now.

Elder Tree: Chuh, I tell yuh bout Miss Cornwall; even if this likkle one was in her family, even if we tree took the child in our arm and went to go visit her, the woman wouldn't be able to tell we yes or no.

Elder One: A true.

Elder Two: She would only say no to avoid responsibility, her and the rest a her jankrow bredrin she always go round with, them all the same.

Elder One: It's not right how Cornwall treat her family.

Elder Two: Not right at all.

Elder Tree: Yuh must raise up yuh own children.

Elder One: If a mama teef with her child tie to her back, then what do you expect of the child?

Elder Two: Yes-I, a lamb take after it mama.

Irie held up her arm and move to come off the table, but I never dare take her; instead, I glance at Elder Tree, who went calmly into her bag and came out with a penny bag of flying saucer. She hand them to Irie without a word and again Irie was content to sit – like magic.

Elder One: No, I can't say I know her face, sister.

Elder Two: I can't neither.

Elder Tree: Come baby, yuh just want some love, don't it?

Elder Tree held out her arm and Irie shuffle to the side of the table and onto the woman lap. A couple of the younger woman try take her, free the elder of the burden, but Elder Tree wouldn't hear it. She send them away to fix the child a plate with a tut, and gradually the people return to them nook and cranny and them own conversation, but still I did stay – waiting and listening.

Elder Two: She a funny thing, isn't she? I only hope her mama don't fret over losing her. I lost I firstborn nuff time.

Elder One: It's a shame bout this here mark.

Elder Two: Yes, it's a shame.

Elder Tree: She too curious.

Elder Two: It's good to be curious.

Elder One: Her mama won't fret if she know anything; girls always come back.

Elder Two: A true, only I girls call I these days.

Elder One: Same here, sister.

Elder Two: I have more son than daughter but still them don't call nearly half as much.

Elder Tree: Why yuh think that is?

Elder One: Society take boy-children from them mama too soon.

Elder Two: Mmmh, Jah create man fi live fi themself and him make woman to live fi man.

Elder One: Jah nah do that, man only tell yuh Him do that.

Elder Tree: Girl put them family first; boy want fi branch out and start them own family.

Elder One: Then them abandon that one too.

Elder Tree: Not all a them, look at Jabari here and Levi.

Elder One: Them all leave one way or another.

Elder Tree: Truth yuh talking still, yuh right.

Elder Two: I remember when I first born I son and him fada come inna the room, first time him come inna the birthing room mind yuh, twice before that when I born him daughter him say him nah come in cos him frighten a the sight of blood. Him say him don't want see I pain, but really him frighten him won't be able to satisfy from I vagina again if him see it like so.

The old woman laugh, the young woman who overstand, blush.

Elder Two: Jah know, the moment I push him son outta I crotch him come and take him from I chest and walk with him to the window. A whole day I spend in labour, yuh know, and the man never come fi comfort him woman, him come fi take him son to the window and show him the street. The boy never cry when him fada hold him. Them stand inna the window and him fada whisper some word inna him ear, and all now I don't know what him tell the boy, and him never say when I did ax him over the years, no matter how much I ax, but from that day I swear the boy was his and his alone. Him walk after him like how duck walk after them mama.

Elder Tree: What the mother them say in Jamaica: 'A fada voodoo with him son and a mama voodoo with her daughter.'

Elder Two: It take only a breast for a boy to feel say him know him mama.

Elder One: Jah make everybody and everything to be in connection with one another. The land, the animal. Then people did mash everything up with them sin and Jah turn Him eye elsewhere. Yuh know sister, sometimes I wonder if this earth was just practice, yuh know? And all the while the people a make up them mind bout who the Almighty-I is, and what Him want from we, but the Almighty-I see what the earth become, what it was turning into, and Him go build a next one some place else and left I&I to it.

The woman laugh again and them never contend no more since Elder One was the most knowledgeable of the tree. Then Irie plate come, and them complain that children her age should be chubby, so she stay with the sisters, and them feed her red pea soup and pieces of okra and plantain, and callaloo, and rice and peas, and she sat there till her belly full. I saw her slip strips of fry plantain inna her pocket when the elders weren't looking, but I couldn't set her straight because them sent I-man upstairs to clean the blood from I face and the cuts on I hands. Them say Miss Nefertari was busy, and it wouldn't be right for her to see I the way I was. Them tell I fi stop landing I-self in trouble, but when I told them that the coppers was the ones what done it, them change up them tune and start insult the buggers like only elders could.

Before I did clean up, I went and poke I head in the kitchen to greet the man. Ganja smoke come from overneath the door, it hurry to fill the house when I did open up. The room was pack. Made smaller by the size of the drum. Made smaller by the movement of the people. I figure the food the woman them was eating must've been prepare elsewhere and brought to the yard with how the kitchen was occupy.

Ras Stephen was closest to the entrance, him touch him chest and we shook hand. Most never register I arrival when I call *Jah*, most were already inna state of trance, heads high, rocking and chanting. Tree man did bang tree drum. A one-two heartbeat rhythm. This was where reggae music start. This, right here in Miss Nefertari kitchen, was the genesis. Not what you might hear pon the radio. The people them head nod in time, experiencing a vibration that brought them to celestial height. A sense of spirituality. A sense of the Almighty-I. What I imagine had start as a counsel, had turn inna time fi worship; an impromptu binghi.

Ras Stephen motion for I to step inside but I only point upstairs to explain why I couldn't. The room was dark and hot, not much light came in through the window; the setting sun was weak. I saw Denton in the corner. Beside him, Ras Joseph led the people in him long dashiki shirt, and him trouser what favour the Muslim wear, and him tall tam. 'I&I people were taken from Africa,' him chant, then the people respond, 'Taken to a foreign land.' Ras Joseph reach behind him and draw Denton inna the miggle of the room. Denton raise up him voice; 'O Iternal Jah,' him say, and the people them follow, 'Grant unto I&I a wise mind.' Ras Joseph was separate to Ras Levi in that him let Denton lead, and Denton always held it over I head. I stand and watch the two of them; fada and son, as Ras Joseph reach out him hand and rest it pon Denton shoulder, and I admit that I did burn a likkle inside, yuh know. I would never admit it out loud, barely would admit it to I-self and give it power, but sometimes I want the closeness what them did have. Denton step back and another man step forward with a book of rebel poems. Ras Joseph lift him head, and him notice I so him wave I inside, but again I only point upstairs and I close the door back. And by the time I made it upstairs, I was glad for the solitude of Miss Nefertari rule.

I went in the bathroom and shut I-self inside. The whole room was pink. The tiles, the shower curtain, the cabinet; even the bath itself was powder pink. We had a mirror cabinet above the sink and for the first time I saw how bad I look. I two eye were near watermelon size, though that was probably because I had dry them so rough. I&I skin was cut, I cheek and neck bruise. Bogey and blood come down from I nose when I pull out the piece of shirt. I wrap it in I tissue and bin it inna the pedal bin beside the toilet. I wash the blood off as best I could and when I was finish I took to sitting on the bath side. Alone with I&I thoughts, some time pass before I realise the drumming stop, though I was glad for it; I want only for the day to be done, but given the elders never know Irie face, there was still the matter of finding her family, and I did want know what the man had decide bout Ras Levi.

I pick up the hand towel and use it to pat I face dry. There was a knock and Miss Nefertari enter. I thought she'd cuss I-man bout the towel, but her face was bright. She tell I that she'd met Irie, and came to know the score. I told her the same half-truth I'd told the woman downstairs. When finish, I ax her how come she was smiling so hard, and she tell I-man that she was happy to have a baby back in the yard.

I grunt and ax: 'What bout Ras Levi, what the brothers them decide?' She tell I-man that none of them wouldn't tell her, but Ras Joseph assure her that a decision had been reach. She tell I that Ras Joseph promise her, with a seriousness in him voice, that soon RastafarI would see the coppers answer for them crime – that it had been a long time coming. 'Is there anything I-man can do?'

'Everybody a leave now,' she say, and she went to stroke I face, before she drew back her hand. 'Everything come back around,' she mutter, 'we're all one wrong bad thing from madness – just look at Job.' She shook the Devil from her shoulder and announce that Irie would spend the night. She tell I that one of the woman had prepare a plate for I-man and it was waiting on the downstairs table where the elders them had left I&I a couple a caramel.

Miss Nefertari saw to Irie. First she run the tap then took her upstairs. I heard her introduce herself as Ras Levi wife – Levi who ran the biggest RastafarI centre in the south of England. I heard her find the plantain hidden in Irie pocket and administer a lecture bout cleanliness proximity to godliness. She put Tosh first record on the player. Turned the tap off. I heard Irie yelp and knew that Miss Nefertari had roll up her sleeve and tested the water with the girl elbow. Miss Nefertari ran some more cold. Still downstairs, I could picture the whole scene. Miss Nefertari would fetch a new flannel and help bathe Irie skin, taking out her hair before seeing to the shampooing and conditioning.

She wrap Irie inna towel once done and had her set the bath for I-man. Miss Nefertari run it till it was full and when I made it to the bathroom, she tell I to see bout I bed as soon as I finish. I lock back the bathroom door, alone again and emptier for it.

I sat in the water, pink smoke surfacing from the cuts in I skin, listening to Miss Nefertari and Irie in the other room if only to keep from thinking bout I failure to protect Makeda. Miss Nefertari was doing the girl hair and using cocoa butter as cream. Again, I could picture the whole affair. She would've had her between her knees, with all her comb and oil line beside her, some of which she wouldn't have taken from them place in the drawer since last she'd use them on I. Her fingers them would've been moving fast through Irie hair, eager to find and feel her root and scalp. She would've had a basin of hot water beside them also, atop tree clean, white towel.

'I want to have my hair soft,' I hear Irie say. 'Like how I seen on TV.'

'Yuh hair not soft already?'

'I mean soft like down, not like Jabari's hair, but down and soft.'

'Yuh hair soft and pretty already, man,' Miss Nefertari said. I imagine she knock the back of Irie head with her comb when she said it, too. I knew how Irie would've been feeling, listening to the low rumbling of Miss Nefertari, because she use fi tend I&I hair the same way. I remember being where Irie was, sitting between her leg, soft reggae music on the radio, her oil finger massaging I head. I remember her telling I&I how the sun in Clarendon was not the same sun that shone elsewhere, how the water was sweet and the fruit shape different. Back in them days, I would look forward to the Sabbath every week, knowing I would be spending time with Miss Nefertari come evening time, but now I&I locs were thick and marga and wild, and Miss Nefertari never ax why I face was mark with cuts and bruises.

In the morning I found Irie at the dining table, where she tell I she love I-man with a mouth full up of breadfruit. I tell her it was bad manners, so she made a game of showing I her half-chew food. Miss Irie was dress in clothes I never recognise and she had a winter coat waiting behind her on her chair back. I ax her where she got the things them from but she never seem fi know – at least she wasn't clear. The yard was clean nah backside as well, as though nobody had pass through last night at all. Miss Nefertari had gone out for the morning, but she'd left one food for I-man. I fetch it from the kitchen and sit beside Irie, hoping to teef what she never finish, but I was glad to see her eat her breadfruit. I nah have no time for the people who said it took the saliva from your mouth, cos I swear there wasn't nothing that grew in Jamaica that I wouldn't consume: mango, ackee, prickly pear, plantain, guava, mammee, chocho, papaya, custard apple and I favourite, sweet potato. Mr Delbert, the newsagent on Frontline for whom I did I paper round, brought them all from Jamaica to St Pauls, whenever them was in season, and him sell them at the Thursday market. It was a blessing, being in foreign, yet eating like we was still in Jamaica. The morning after the night Mr Delbert receive a shipment, Miss Nefertari and the rest a the woman in St Pauls would arrive at the gates of the makeshift market-place before dawn. On those market days, I would rise to hear Miss Nefertari singing pure roots and rocksteady as she sort her green leaf from her pears.

On one of those same market-day morning, right after fin-ishing a plate of breadfruit and ackee, I remember axing Ras Levi, who was sat across from I, why Rasta couldn't repatriate back to Jamaica instead of Ethiopia. I told him how I want to see Clarendon; May Pen and the Rio Minho. I member how Miss Nefertari stop her singing and Ras Levi set him fork down pon the table and ax: 'Why yuh want know that for, Jabari?' And him eye them were full of fire, but him face were calm, which frighten I more than if him was mad. I knew I say something wrong, but never know what, so I never mention wanting to see the place where him grow, thinking something sentimental might vex him further. I look to Miss Nefertari, but this did happen after there was already a rupture in our relationship, so she never look back, instead she fuss herself with her blouse. Fighting panic, I tell I papa that I only ax because I never want fi stop eating our food – I gesture at the breadfruit.

Ras Levi never speak for a second. Him had him elbow pon the table and clasp him hands in front a him face. Him tell I how everything that grow in Jamaica grow in Ethiopia too. Him say most of the food we eat inna the West Indies

117

was brought from Africa along the same passage we were. How Jamaica was a land drench in blood and was never fi we land to begin with. Him say only a Day-by-Day see Jamaica as a place of significance, only them who never overstand the importance of having an ancestral land . . . of having a home and belonging someplace. Then him return to him breakfast and Miss Nefertari went back to her singing, although her song did change for something sadder than before.

Soon as we finish, I help Irie arm through her coat and we were out Miss Nefertari yard. With the fresh morning air and Irie atop I shoulder again I felt like her papa – and it was a good feeling too, like I had responsibility and some place to go, like somebody passing might look at I-man and think I was dropping I&I yute off at the community creche before heading a work. Irie was chipper as well, probably because her clothes were fresh and her hair wasn't so stiff: I could smell the pomade Miss Nefertari use. She was going on bout the next time she visit Miss Nefertari yard and the things she couldn't wait to do with I&I again. She carry on talking till we reach Frontline and found the Mother Earth dark and close.

I knock and we did wait. A proper café would've been open in the early morning, ready to feed the tradesmen and the returning night-shift workers, but the Mother never operate like a regular caf – the few time I'd seen it open earlier than midday was when it hadn't close the night before.

There had only been two month between Joyce Kelly leaving the centre and her opening the café. It was empty before she move in, a husk of a shop on Frontline; before that it was a print shop, before that, no one could rightly remember. No one knew where Joyce and Angela get them money neither. The people did speculate, it was barbershop gossip, but them could never say for sure, and of course neither Joyce nor Angela would answer – I imagine them did enjoy the attention the hearsay brought.

All the people knew for sure was that one minute the shop was nothing, and the next it was another beating heart in St Pauls. Joyce took members of the centre along with her when she left – people convince by her slick words that denounce RastafarI as a man club. Soon after she open, she start a newspaper in which she write that RastafarI woman suffer subordination in the midst of liberation movement – that black woman were the downpress of the downpress – then she did pay a couple yutes from the Gardens to post it through everybody letterbox.

When Ras Levi read it, him and Enoch did take a couple of the bigger Rases to straighten things out, but them were met by about twenty people, man and woman, who fold them arm and twist up them face and wouldn't allow the Iyamen inside. The newspaper was still running to this day; it had more pages, and adverts too, though I wasn't sure Joyce contribute to the writing anymore, and now the yutes from the Gardens avoid RastafarI yard on them route. I still saw the paper on the sill of Mr Delbert shop, and I did flick through it from time to time, and sometimes it make sense – when them was talking bout white people and the sufferation them cause – but as soon as them start talk bout black woman as somehow separate

119

from the black man, I tune out, iyah. I prefer them to continue speaking against the coppers them, because we would always have that in common, but as Angela demonstrate, them did often take it further than RastafarI – not because we was frighten, nothing can't trouble RastafarI – only because our ambition did differ, we want fi leave, and them want fi carve themself a piece a England.

The Mother run them affair separate to I&I as well: them never have a pardna like how we did, instead them make them money in the caf. Day-by-Day people would often be found in attendance: woman would attend for the library them had at the back of the shop, as well as for them reading group and them nursery; and like Makeda say, if a woman in the community, like Pearl or Miss Francis, did have some expertise inna certain field, like theatre or politics, then she could pitch a lesson idea to Joyce and she would be able to set up her own classes. The man who frequent the Mother went to drink and chat and play domino and Ludi; a few went because them politics align; and some because them did want fi be near them girlfriend. So despite being smaller than the centre it was often busier, and to I&I it seem more a social club than a social organisation.

I swear, every Babylon narrative surrounding St Pauls was born outta the Mother Earth: the colour pimps who kept white whore, unlicense liquor, illegal gambling, affray and red-flag communism. There wasn't a crime or indecency that the Mother Earth hadn't been link to, or raid under the suspicion of, but from the outside looking in, you never would've thought it was the source of such disquiet. It look respectable enough. It have big shop windows and a new door, and the sign that swung from the side was tidy. It have a flat roof, which, had it been in St Andrews, would've had chairs and a table, and the table would've had a purple tablecloth and tall candlesticks. Joyce did fancy herself as something of a florist, so the café was ram with hanging plants and flowerpots, and she kept two bushes in basins out front beside next pots full of label plants: freesias, morning glory and foxtail lilies. Potted chrysanthemums and monkshood were join by cheap metal tables and chairs. The flowers and plants were either grown on the allotment slopes, or them were brought in from the surrounding county. RastafarI was a pathway to nature, and though the café activity were far from RastafarI ideals, the livity had seep inna the soil of what it was to be Jamaican, and the two were often confuse.

It was always the first place anyone visit after finishing stretches inside. I remember when a number of people were release round the same time and Joyce threw a welcome-home party. Denton and I happen to be passing that night on patrol, and Denton nod at one of the many man out front. Him tell I&I not to stare so hard. 'Yuh see that one there so with the trilby? Baba tell I that him have that long scar behind him ear from where him get cut outside a pub over Easton.' Then him point at a thick-eyebrow woman who laugh like a starting car. 'See that one there, she end up inna prison fi kill her husband, did it with a skillet: madwoman.'

You hear all sorts of rumour bout the people who frequent

the café; most were nonsense, of course – but some were bound to be true. The empress them at the Cultural and Community Centre tell we that them did recruit yutes from the home and the Gardens and had them climb through house window up a Clifton. Them say Joyce only water her plant so the leaves would cover the window and no one couldn't see what was going on inside, and I swear the sistrens would've had more than a couple things to say if them had known I was bringing Irie there. I knock on the curtained, glass door again and another few minute pass before Joyce deign to answer.

8

Joyce told I to come in and be quick bout it. I went to complain, saying how the cold wasn't good for pickney, but she told I to shut I mouth. Since Makeda had first begun coming to the café, Joyce and I had reach something of an armistice. The Mother Earth nah shake I-man like it did the rest of the yutes from the centre; if I was looking for Makeda I would barge inside, don't matter whether it was a regular day, whether them had a woman meeting, whether it was crowded or empty, nobody couldn't say nothing— I went in with I head high and I locs brandish. The only word the two of we exchange were bout Makeda: where she was, or when she would be back from wherever she had gone. I wouldn't never forget I manners when we talk, but Joyce never said *please* or *thank you:* she talk how she want and did as she please.

There weren't a woman more famous in St Pauls, probably in the whole of the city. No one knew exactly how old she was, and she claim not to know herself, but Makeda imagine she was somewhere in her forties . . . or fifties. Joyce tell Makeda that it nah matter how old her birth certificate rule her because she still look young and sexy. The only reason Makeda figure she was any older than thirty was cos she was always going on bout things in the past as if she'd been there. She was mampy, with broad shoulder, and when she comb her fro out, she look bigger still. When she did shout her voice travel right the way down Frontline and into the Gardens, and the pigeons them fly from the road and go nest someplace quieter.

The inside of the Mother Earth was separate inna two room, both brought the outside in: calendula and Michaelmas daisy were pack in small vessel and arrange pon table. The first room was the café area itself, which held the table and the chair, a couple radio – one of which, set high upon a tall shelf, was playing lovers rock low – and the Ludi board and the patty oven, all of which sat on the counter beside the till, and a sink and a green Buddha and shelf of tatter paperback and pamphlet. It shelf was full of cookbook and orchid. Any spare space was fill with flora: senecio, trailing rosemary and English ivy hung from hook and high sills. Herbs were pot by the stove so that them could be pluck and use while cooking, the plates were made from bagasse, and the regulars bounce herb and cigarette smoke from the ceiling. The second, slightly smaller, back room was where Joyce kept all her coffee bean and tea leaf and small packet of Shirley biscuit, which she had Mr Delbert ship direct from Barbados, and her plant pots and tree ram bookcase that made up the community library; she only stock book written by black and Coolie woman. The whole place favour a greenwood with its many flowerpot, and the high ceiling was cover by a mesh wire which had more ivy growing round and between, and them did brush against your face when you walk inside. Immediately Irie went to feel them. I told her to look but not touch.

Makeda was sat at one of the table, the same kind that was out front, that you might find at a garden centre. She was in the same trouser and shoe as the day before, the same big jacket, pair with a red turtleneck this time. She call good morning to Irie and came to take her from I-man, but before she could, Joyce took hold of the likkle girl face and turn her head to expose her birthmark. She appraise it for a second or two before she went into the back room – turning the radio power off as she pass.

'I guess yuh tell her already?' I said, and Makeda nod. 'Yuh tell her everything?'

'Yeah. I thought she could help, init. But she inna bad mood, man, chuh.'

'Because of this?'

'Because of Angela, me tell yuh already. Well, because of Angela and probably this now as well. I don't know for sure, but either way the woman vex, man.' Makeda went to the front door and lock it behind we. She reach for the hanging plants that cover the window and check the road. She may have left the centre, but her mama had still forbidden her from setting foot in the Mother Earth – she tell her it was where the man who love woman too much and the woman who love man went – but it was too late: Makeda had found something in Joyce, a woman she'd always seen saying whatever she want and going wherever she please, with a blunt in her mouth, gold jewellery round her neck, in her ear and pon every finger, gulping Colt 45s with a coarse tongue. I imagine Joyce was how Makeda imagine her namesake, a woman who'd overseen a business that move by way of land with many caravan, and on sea by many ship. One who trade with merchants of Indian and Nubian and Aswân lineage. Who open negotiation with a man like King Solomon for supply of gold, ebony and sapphire. Try as I might, I could never convince her back into Rasta, and I knew Joyce was the reason too. Joyce return with a small and mash up book in her hand. 'So yuh recognise her, then Joyce?' Makeda say. 'Yuh seen the birthmark, yeah?'

Joyce never answer at first, she sit at a table and tell I fi take Irie and find her something to do upstairs. She said she must speak to I&I alone a moment. I took Irie up the stairs, which were sandwich between the front and back room, and open the door to Joyce one-bed flat. I'd never been above the café before, but the place was divide inna a living room, kitchen, bathroom and bedroom, and each branch from the same short hallway. It was more cramp than downstairs. I set Irie at a foldable dining table and found her a biro and some old bills on the kitchen side to draw on. She could amuse herself, and if she get bored, well I don't business whether she wreck anything, anyway.

'I know the girl mama. The city took Irie, and the rest of her mama yute as well,' said Joyce, soon as I was back downstairs, sitting at the table with her and Makeda. 'Her name Cedella, she use to live in Easton, over St George way, but she move a while ago.'

'It's the birthmark, init,' Makeda say. She slap the tabletop like she a shout domino. 'That's how yuh knew her face, init? See Jabari, I told yuh Joyce would know her, man. We should've come here from the start, bredrin.'

'I knew *somebody* was bound fi recognise her,' I said.

Joyce suck her teeth. 'It's not a birthmark, it's a scar – a burn.'

'A burn?' Makeda ax, and suddenly the elders remark bout the mark being a shame make a ton a sense.

'Listen,' Joyce said, and when she did move forward her chair scrape against the concrete floor and make a terrible sound. 'This is what's going to happen from here on out, me nah want discuss anything more bout what unuh done, what unuh think unuh plans are, how unuh think I could help, or nothing else. Me nah want fi hear yuh twopence, Jabari, cos I can see yuh itching to open yuh mouth and talk. But the time fi talk is done. Makeda already tell me everything me need fi know and my mind already made. I want that likkle girl outta my shop as soon as possible, but yuh need fi learn something first.'

'Which is what?'

'Me tell yuh me know the girl mother, me tell yuh she move but me still know where she there: me a go take unuh now.'

'To Irie mama?'

'Yes.'

'Now?'

'Right now. Get yuh things them ready,' she say. I look pon Makeda, triumphant, but Joyce shut we down. 'This is not a day trip,' she say. 'This is the chance for unuh to learn the way things are' – she fix her eye pon I-man – 'and the right way to go bout changing them. Go and fetch the girl,' she said, and Makeda hurry off before she could change her mind. I follow Joyce into the backroom where she collect her coat and things. Upstairs, I could hear Makeda chasing Irie bout the place.

'Yo, Joyce, was Angela seriously going to blow up the bank on City Road?' I ax, and Joyce pause with one arm in her coat. She search I face for something, but she never find nothing. She fed her other arm through her sleeve and refuse fi answer before Makeda did return with Irie. Then she cut her eye after I-man and we did climb inna her vehicle, which was park in the alley behind the café.

Weston-super-Mare was a dump of a beach town, but it had a pier and a Ferris wheel and it was a favourite destination of the poorer schools in the city. I'd been once before, when Orville Mann did fall inna the water and our teacher went after him. I remember tree old white man sat pon a bench did laugh and buss joke bout Orville drowning. It was the first time I'd left Bristol without Ras Levi, and it reaffirm everything him had ever said bout white people devilry. Our teacher fish Orville from the water and give the white man a piece of her mind, but them only carry on anyway. We weren't allow on school trips after that, so some yutes saw to leaving Orville outta the game pon the playground.

Joyce park overneath the Ferris wheel. It wasn't a warm day, so the stone beach was barren, but it wasn't chilly neither, so Joyce give Makeda some pocket money and tell her fi take Irie for candy floss and ice cream and to meet we back at the car in an hour. I could tell Makeda want to argue, but it was clear that Joyce nah ramp, so Makeda flounce toward the pier and Irie ran ahead of her, pointing at the wheel and the water, talking bout mint ice cream and wishing Makeda was as animated as she was. I try fi lift Makeda mood by shouting something bout not falling into the water like Orville Mann, but I don't think she heard. Irie did. She laugh after I and shout that I was silly.

That's the trouble with yutes – everything is new and exciting and them stoke all the time. And as an adult, you try your best to match them energy, despite the fact that you still see and hear the old buggers what was laughing at Orville. And sometimes you manage it, but sometimes you never, and when you never, the poor yute start to think that perhaps the world wasn't all that exciting, and them stop laugh half as much.

Joyce and I set off for Cedella yard. After a five-minute walk, we turn inna one housing estate and immediately I overstood why Joyce did park elsewhere. The first thing we see was a Cortina without tyres, prop up on a pile a brick with bin bag for window. There were a ton of bike on the people them driveway and Joyce say that's what yutes round Makeda and I age did round here: them nick car, chopper, moped, any-thing with wheel and a engine. The few people we see look as though them did trawl through them neighbour rubbish on Christmas Eve, hoping for a telltale package. After another five minute, Joyce come to a halt outside one of the maison-ette. She consult the tatter book she pick up earlier and in it I seen a scribble address written on its last page. She declare that we were here, and the yard was indistinguishable from its neighbours.

'Come,' Joyce say, and I follow her to the front door. 'She need some flowers out front,' she go on.

Usually, when you call upon a home in St Pauls, you hear pickney on the other side shouting that there was someone at the door, and then someone else shouting for someone else to answer it. You heard the scratching of small hands reaching for the lock, or music, or laughter, or anger, but outside of Cedella yard I couldn't hear nothing at all. Then come a shuffling of feet, then a voice, rough and presumptive, axing who it was.

'It's Joyce, Cedella, from the Mother Earth. Me have someone me want fi introduce yuh to.' Silence. 'Cedella, if yuh don't open this door my sister . . .'. When finally, Cedella did, she was in her dressing gown and slippers, her straighten hair tie up inna old rag. Ras Levi would've had a heart attack if Miss Nefertari ever answer the door like that. Joyce never make a fuss though. She pull Cedella inna hug, like say them was the best of friend. She say how good it was to see her and push her way inside. After that, Cedella never have much of a choice but to invite I&I to sit.

She ax who I was and before I-man could speak, Joyce explain that I was Ras Levi boy, to which Cedella laugh and ax what I was doing with Joyce. As the two woman talk, I did study her. She hold her full lips apart when she listen. Her breath smelt a drink. Her eye were black but flat, and period-ically, she reach to itch the back of her neck. I found Irie in the way she held her mouth and how fast she spoke. Right then,

I want to come out with everything, tell her that we had her daughter and we want to give her back. But I held my tongue, not only because of Cedella discomfort, but the place was a mess. And not a comfortable mess neither, like how some a them inna the Gardens live, where the lights never work when you need them, and nozzles were held in alliance with taps by tape. It wasn't the kind of mess that make you feel at ease, it was the kind that meant you never want sit down. The glass coffee table was crack and stain with rings, too low for the sofa. The carpet was worn. Empty bokkle of cheap wine and spirit were strewn about. The lights them did blink. I said no when Cedella offer a cup of tea. Joyce said yes and we follow her through the living room to the kitchen, which was just as mash up as the living room. 'City was meant to send someone to fix that,' Cedella said, but I never know to what she was referring because I-man could count at least five things that did need fixing – a couple of the cupboard units did look as though them might come off the wall with a tug. 'City don't send no people round no coloured house.'

'How're the yutes?' Joyce ax.

Cedella fill the kettle and put it down on the heat. 'I hear they're alive, Joyce, I hear they're surviving,' she say, in an accent closer to farmland English than Jamaican. 'Just like their mother is. Just like we all are, aren't we?'

'You speak to them much?'

'The ones I'm allow to, I speak to, yeah. When I'm allow to, I speak to them.'

'How's living out here been? Lonely, I imagine.'

131

'It is, yeah,' Cedella said. She fold her arm and lean back against the countertop while the old kettle did whistle. The two woman face off. 'Nobody from home hasn't come visit me since I left, not even you Joyce, despite you all clearly knowing where I am. I thought you would've forgotten after all this time.'

In response, Joyce lift the book with Cedella address written inside.

'I assumed you'd lost it,' Cedella say. It was like I was no longer in the room. Cedella smile and restart. 'Well, to answer your question, the neighbours keep putting shit through my door. Literal shit, I mean. Bags of it after they take their dogs out for a walk, and their dogs fucking bark all hours of night. I hear them saying things as well. White people get real nasty when they want you gone. I didn't have no choice but to come out here, though. Wasn't like the city spread out a big map of Bristol in front of me and gave me a choice. Never had nothing called choice my whole life. Didn't have a choice when they took my yutes and my house from me, now the city want me to be grateful out here surrounded by these white bastards. I hear they're talking about letting us buy these places for cheap. Who'd want them, that's why.'

She swivel and phlegm inna her sink. She ran the hot tap to swill it into the sewers before facing Joyce once more, her wild eye almost daring her to judge. 'I wish we had a word for white people the same way Americans do. A word like cracker or honkey to call them. It probably wouldn't do them nothing, don't have no weight behind it, no history behind it, and it's the history behind them what makes people feel words, isn't it? But still it feel good to say sometimes, you know? They got plenty of words for us.' She turn to I. 'I remember your papa liked words.'

Joyce laugh, a short cynical bark that never break the tension but only made the room stranger. 'Levi don't have no love for words less him the one saying them.'

I went to retaliate, but Cedella got there first. 'You always loved your words too, didn't you, Joyce?' she said, and I seen life in her eye. 'I remember you had all them cases of books you'd let the woman come and borrow. They was all written by coloured woman, weren't they? I remember I borrowed a few in my time, including that one there that I wrote my address in, init. Actually, I probably still have a couple of them lying around someplace, if I didn't leave them in the last house.' Cedella shuffle her bum along the counter edge, her feet still pon the kitchen tile. She reach her hand out and Joyce give her the book. I thought the room might explode if them hand touch, but Joyce hand her one end and Cedella took the opposite corner. Cedella bent the spine, lick her finger and flick through the page. Then she tear the page that held her address from the book, fold it and put it inna her back pocket before she return the book back to Joyce. Behind her, steam burst from the kettle. 'What bout Angela? She ain't here with you? She outside in the car?'

'Angela is fine.'

'That's good,' Cedella say, and there was something in the way she say it that made I-man pay even greater attention.

She found a foil bokkle cap on the floor and kick it between her toes. Nothing change in her eye, I was looking, she kept them averted, but her voice took a turn; it became wistful. 'You and her was always close, I liked that bout unuh, you don't see many friends stay so close as you. I hear she get lock up? Something bout a bank?'

'Something like that,' Joyce say.

'That's why she's not here, init? She was always a fiery one. The one that want to pick up a tyre iron and go sort everyone's problems.' She pause. 'Sometimes I found she was a likkle too inna though, you know, Joyce?'

'How yuh mean?' Joyce said, but something gave I-man the feeling that she knew exactly what Cedella meant. I had the impression too that the visit was no longer in Joyce hand, that she had come meaning for it to be one thing, but now Cedella was making it another. She was an unpredictable woman, that much was clear. I never rest I footback pon the floor; I did stay pon I toe, ready to move.

'I don't know,' Cedella said, playing a game. 'But she used to go on like she was better than people with the way she'd hand out advice for free. I remember she try it on me a couple of times and I had to tell her bout herself, man. I brought her house into it, I told her mines wasn't like hers in the Gardens, man. It wasn't some social housing thing. My neighbours weren't drunks. I told her to look at where she lived; she wasn't better than no one, least of all me. Remember I knew Angela from before she start going round with you. Me and her was close them times, but after I said what I said bout her

134

place she weren't having it no more – we fell out. The bank though – shit. I always knew she had something like that in her. Something wild. She used to put me on edge when she got in one of her moods, man. Couple times I was afraid to speak my mind round her, but then I just snapped outta it, you know? I was a lot more afraid in them days.' She lift her head. 'I was afraid of you as well.'

'Of me?' Joyce smile. 'Why? Me always like yuh. I thought we got on well.'

Cedella return to the cap. 'A lot of people were frightened of you in those days.'

'Rubbish.'

'No, they was. I remember.'

'Well, them shouldn't've been.'

'Yeah, there are a lot more terrible things in the world than you, Joyce. It was silly really, but I'm younger than you and Angela, don't forget. I was a lot more impressionable and naive them times. Things kinda went over my head then, but I've had a lot of time to sit and think bout that time in my life, you know?'

Joyce point behind her. 'The kettle boil,' she say.

Cedella nah move. 'I've had a lot of time to think, think bout everything that used to go over my head back in them days there, and I've reached the conclusion that Angela's not a good person, you know, Joyce. That's what I've come to realise. She didn't speak life into people, and the books I'm reading these days say you must speak life, you know. There's too much doubt around; too much doubt and death.'

'What book yuh a read, maybe I could borrow some if yuh have a couple spare?' Joyce say, but Cedella would not sway.

'I remember when me and Angela used to go round together, before either of us met you, I guess you must've been with Levi in the centre, being a good girl, whereas me and Angela, we was running the streets, man: getting into all sorts. It was Angela's mouth getting us into things them days there, you know what I'm talking bout. She could either put it on you and make you feel like you could climb a mountain, or make you feel like you didn't want to get outta bed. She knew that. I watched her do it. But them days her mouth was fun, watching her use it against other people: the men we came across, and the women too.' She laugh. 'At first she never hurt me with it, she told me I was hers – that no one couldn't trouble me. I believed her, you know, that's the kind of girl I was: impressionable, like I said. And that's the kind of woman she is, init? But you know that better than anyone. She'll tell you something and you'll just believe it, init? Don't matter how extravagant it is.' Cedella crush the bokkle cap overneath her foot and cross the room, taking milk from the fridge, behind her the cap did spring back inna shape. 'So how did it go with the bank exactly? Did she tell you she was going to do it, or did she just go head and do it anyway?'

'I don't know nothing bout no bank, Cedella.' Joyce say. 'It's a conspiracy. Them want her for some other crime, I reckon.' She lick her lips.

Cedella squat in front of a cabinet and took two tea bag

from a box of five hundred. She did rock a likkle when she crouch, but still she was impressively stable for a woman who'd been on the bokkle. Thought she might've stayed in this state so she was use to it. 'Oh come off it, Joyce,' she say. 'Maybe the crackers do want her for something else as well, but as soon as I heard bout the bank, I knew it was true. She's like that isn't she, Angela? She wants to be in the mix up – wants what's exciting and drops it when it isn't.' She rise and slosh the bag and the milk in two mug. 'You know what I reckon happened? I bet she came to you with the idea and you told her not to be stupid, told her to drop it – that she'd go down. I bet she looked you in your eye and told you she would drop it, didn't she? How much sugars you want?'

'Just the one,' Joyce say tightly, and when Cedella hand her the tea, she set it down. 'And how bout yuh work, how's that these days?'

'Work's the same,' Cedella say. She warm her hand with the hot drink a few inches from her face, blowing the surface and staring into it.

'Yuh know I ran into one of yuh yute, Cedella. That's why me even think to come check yuh all of a sudden.'

'Which one?'

'The likklest one.'

'Oh yeah?'

'Yeah, man. I did meet her new parents, what them call? the Ro—'

'Roskillys. They're up in St Andrews.'

'Oh, so yuh know already? I thought Irie was one of the

137

children yuh weren't supposed to see? That's why me come fi tell yuh.'

'I know where all of my children are.'

'I can respect that.'

Cedella face flash upwards. 'I'm not after your respect, Joyce. Never have been.'

Joyce took a moment, wait for Cedella to return to her hot drink. 'Yuh know, seeing Irie remind me of the night when yuh come by the caf; the night she get burn.'

Cedella reach inna drawer: inside she had only a dessert spoon, a knife, a fork and two kitchen knives; one big, one small. The loose cutlery rattle against the drawer side with how she open it so aggressive. She reach for the dessert spoon. 'What you trying to do, Joyce?' She kept her head at a slight angle, neither looking at Joyce directly, nor looking away. Still I did shift pon I feet, glancing between the two woman.

'Me? Me nah try nothing.'

'Yuh want bring Levi yute inna my yard and try embarrass me?' Her head was still held askew. Her voice wilder. More Jamaican. 'Me know yuh do. Yuh want fi bring him round unannounce so that me nah have time fi clean up, bringing up that night and my yutes and shit?' She swap between Bristol and wherever her family come from backayard. Her anger in the driver seat. 'I know what kinda woman you and Angela are: the two a yuh spiteful. I know you're trying to catch me with my pussy out, but I don't give a fuck, yuh hear? I don't give a fuck if my pussy's out. I'll show the world my shit: it's the world what give it me.'

'Me nah try do nothing,' Joyce say again, but Cedella was off.

'You don't think I regret what happen? You don't think I think about it? You can't do nothing to me, Joyce.' She turn on I-man. The drawer was still open behind her. 'Yuh want fi know what happen, Levi yute? One accident happen, that's what happen, because everybody make mistake and everybody has accident, and I went to this woman here that night thinking I had a friend who understood that.' She level a finger in Joyce direction, either her drunkenness or her vexation causing her to miss by a couple shades. 'Thinking that as a woman who supposedly had dedicated her life to helping coloured woman, that she would help.' Her voice shatter. I could tell she was replaying the night in her head, that she wasn't really looking at, nor talking to I-man, but rather she was seeing Frontline, or the Gardens, or whatever she did see that there night. 'I knew me and Angela had had our falling-out by then,' she continue, 'but still I thought she was big enough to put that over there, you know, behind her. But no, she wasn't no help at all, and now she's here, for sport, bringing the past up and dashing it back in my fucking face like I won't fucking cut her.'

'I wasn't no help?'

Cedella was on fire, she round on her. 'No, you weren't.'

'If me nah take Irie then, she would be dead right now.'

'It wasn't that bad, man.'

'Try blame me, Cedella,' Joyce said, her coolness slipping. 'It was yuh one who left her to pull the pan from the stove, and it was yuh who should've taken her to the hospital, but yuh was too frighten them would snitch to the coppers and them would come take yuh child, so yuh bring her to me and I did fix her up and keep her the night. Me look after her like say she was mine. Me even ax if yuh want stay too, but yuh went go back out instead, back to yuh work. And when I bring her to yuh inna the morning, yuh tell me fi keep her. Yuh say that. Yuh look pon yuh own daughter and couldn't face what yuh done, so yuh tell me fi keep her, Cedella. Yuh one do that.'

'And you're here to remind me of that, yeah? My own personal angel with the book of names held open and ready to judge. You're not so holy. And me never go back a work that night. Yuh wrong. I went back to the house to look after the rest of Irie sibling.'

Joyce shake her head. 'That's a damn lie and we both know it.'

'It's the truth.'

'I know it's a lie because Angela see yuh in the Gardens after yuh did leave.'

'Oh *Angela* – because Angela tell yuh it must be true.'

'It is true.'

'And what was our friend doing up that late, where was she going, mmh?'

'Come Jabari, we're done,' Joyce said. She march from the kitchen, her tea still untouch and I went after her, cept I never turn I&I back on Cedella because I knew say the knife drawer was still open – either Joyce hadn't notice or she was braver than I.

'What yuh come here for, Joyce?' Cedella say, following after I&I. 'After all this here time, what yuh come here for?'

'To see if anything change,' Joyce call over her shoulder. She open the door and only when we were outta the house did I turn I back and skip to her side.

Behind we, Cedella hysteria follow we through the estate, ignorant of the white faces that did appear in her neighbour windows. 'Yuh can't judge me, Miss Perfect,' she yell. 'Yuh can't judge me. I asked you to keep her but you didn't want to, don't come to me because you feel guilty now that you seen her in St Andrews with two crackers. Don't fucking come feel guilty round me. I know they live in one of those big yards in St Andrews. I been up there. I seen them. I know Irie don't think bout me. I wouldn't think about me if I had all what she got. I know where all of my children are, Joyce. Where are yours? We all know why you don't have none of your own, don't we, Joyce? The whole of St Pauls know!'

We turn the corner and were soon outta the rotten estate. 'That's not what me want fi happen,' Joyce say. 'Me never expect her fi go after me like that and me lose it. Me sorry yuh affi see that, Jabari.'

'It's cool,' I say back. 'Yuh nah affi apologise.'

If it was a summer day we might've heard the local tourist at the beach from where we were a few streets away, but much like Cedella yard, there wasn't nothing. I wait a minute before the silence grew too much, so I ax why Cedella was like that.

'Like what?'

'Mad.'

'Why's anybody like anything? Yuh expect her fi be normal when Irie like how she is?' Joyce was still walking so fast I affi skip, and she wouldn't look at I-man when she speak neither. She was looking up at the big wheel in the distance, up at the sky.

'Like what. Slow, you mean?'

'No, not slow. Yuh nah notice how as soon as she come in the door she try hug me? Yuh nah notice that? She was talking fast too.'

'Yeah, I notice, man. I just thought she was being friendly – that's all.'

'It's a survival thing,' she say, but not inna mean tone. It was probably the most straightest she'd ever spoke to I-man. 'She don't know she doing it, but she was tryna get pon my good side, yuh know. See if I'm a danger or not.'

I guess it made sense; Irie was certainly like that with everybody I'd seen her round. And I remember Makeda did say something similar. 'Why Cedella ax yuh where yuh yutes there?' I continue. 'Yuh lost them to the city too?'

'I never had no children to lose.' We reach the car before Makeda and Irie. Joyce sat pon the bonnet and I stood, but still she did avoid I sight.

'So what she a talk bout? Saying how she knows why yuh never have none?'

She turn up her jacket collar. 'She must be mad, like how yuh say. Yuh nah cold?'

'I'm all right,' I say. 'Yuh don't want none? No yute?'

142

'Me neither want them nor don't, maybe I will sometime, but right now it would mean giving up on all my work, putting the needs of one over many.' She check her shoulder, probably wishing for Makeda to appear with Irie soon so we could leave. It wasn't a nice place, Weston. You did feel on edge there as a black person. There were probably tons of National Front nearby – inside police uniform and out. Them was probably the people putting the shit through Cedella door. It weren't the warmest of welcome inna Cedella yard, to put it mildly, but if I did live alone pon that estate I might open the door with a one cutlass inna I hand – so I couldn't judge, really.

'A black woman should have children, still,' I said, wanting to move I mind from any thought of the National Front and I&I vulnerability. 'It's a black woman responsibility.'

Joyce grunt as if I did tell an unfunny joke. 'So yuh people say.'

'Is that why yuh nah take Irie? Cos yuh don't want none?'

She take out a cigarette and start fi smoke. She must've been smoking her whole life she smoke it so fast. 'One of the reason,' she go, and the smoke went all round we inna billow with how fast she done it.

'Yuh could take her now, though? If yuh regret not doing that? Get yuh people to help out if it too much. Balance it between all a unuh?' I wave the cigarette smell from in front of I nose; I never overstood why people smoke cigarette when ganja exist. Jah never make cigarette.

'Them them own people,' Joyce say. 'I can't tell them fi raise a child.'

'Yeah, but yuh a the leader init.'

'We don't have no leader. We have a committee, we vote for members, we vote for everything what we do. We don't operate like how yuh papa operate.'

'There has to be a leader, otherwise nothing would get done.'

'Ras Levi unuh leader?'

'Of course.'

'I thought Haile Selassie was the only leader?' Some life come back inna her voice, so I knew she was trying to poke I button.

I tut. 'Obviously His Imperial Majesty is the one true leader, but Ras Levi is our leader while we here in St Pauls – overs?'

'Who make him the leader?' She took more interest in the conversation now.

'I don't know. It was before I-man was born; Jah maybe.'

'Well we don't have a leader, like I said. We vote.'

'So did unuh vote on blowing up the bank?'

Her eyelid did narrow. 'Everybody them own person: that's the strength of having a committee. We never silence nobody; some of we believe in direct action, some of we believe in slow action, but none of we believe in running. And me tell yuh already, same way me tell Cedella, me nah know nothing bout no bank.' She flick her butt inna the road and reach for another from her packet. She open the top, pick one out with her teeth, then slip the packet back inna her pocket, withdrawing her hand with her lighter same time. There was a smoothness to the things she did do, I won't lie. She saw I-man watching her and ax if I did mind. I said I never, not because it was true, but because I knew she was going to light it anyway.

'I know why yuh bring I-man here as well,' I said. 'I know yuh want I-man to see how mash up Cedella is, so I wouldn't want fi bring Irie back here. Yuh want we fi take Irie back to St Andrews, don't it?'

Joyce suck her draw. 'Yutes can't imagine growing old, and the old forget what it mean to be young. But not me, me still remember how it is: me know yuh need fi see it otherwise yuh never would've listen. Now yuh know why Irie can't go back there, init. The city get a lot of things wrong. Them even mishandle some case like this one: but this one them get right.'

'If Irie was I&I baby,' I said after a brief quiet, 'I would never let no liarsment man come take her.'

Makeda and Irie appear at the road end. 'Yuh hear what Cedella say when me ax how she was?' Joyce say. She held her new cigarette all dainty and stare at its end. 'She said that in spite of everything . . . she was alive. Survival is the most everyday form of resistance, my yute. Whether right or wrong, Cedella have an answer for everybody who would see her fail, no matter what yuh think a her; and yuh affi admire that.' She took another drag. 'Personally, me always did admire mothers for not being scared of how easy it is for something to go wrong with them pickney. Children are so delicate, yuh know. I've always been afraid of that.'

When Irie arrive, she run inna I arm and I did sweep her high inna the sky, answering her question bout where Joyce and I had been with lies.

9

Joyce drive we back to the Mother Earth, where she tell we fi lock the door and left. She return in an hour, after twilight. By which time I'd catch Makeda up to speed and we was playing card game pon the upstairs dining table. Irie was in front of the box, her head lolling into her chest – she'd soon be asleep. Joyce come and tell we fi leave Irie so we did follow her downstairs to where she had yard food waiting. She switch the radio on. Freddie McGregor sang. She slip her hand inna glove and proceed fi tend her plants them as we sat and ate: trimming, rehousing and scribbling new labels with a lopsided style. 'I've been St Andrews,' she say, matter-of-fact, 'met with Mrs Roskilly.'

'What?' I said, mouth open, a forkful of brown stew somewhere between it and the box in which it come. 'Why'd you do that for?' I put the food aside and never trouble it again.

'How yuh find them?' Makeda said, equally confuse.

'I follow the "missing" poster, ax round – all them neighbour seem to think very highly of them. Me give them a fake name, tell them me run a charity working with battered woman down a St Pauls, say me hear bout Irie from a friend and want to offer our support – it's the same thing me tell Mrs Roskilly when them eventually direct me to her front door. She was a bit funny with me at first, Mrs Roskilly, but with all that's happen, it make sense, still. It's a nice yard them have: big, too big for me, and them have gravel instead a grass, but it nice same way. Her husband was out looking for Irie, so Mrs Roskilly was home alone, manning the phone. Poor woman, she look like she never sleep at all, bredda. Me can't imagine what she feeling.'

'So what?' I said. I was angry. 'Cedella look like she never sleep neither. Why yuh a even travel there anyway? Makeda and I were talking before yuh come back. We were gonna wait till Ras Levi come home before we decide anything and now yuh gone and done this, man, chuh.'

The snapping of Joyce scissors did punctuate the following silence. 'I took unuh into Weston to meet Cedella so yuh could know what I know. I went into St Andrews to see the same thing what unuh had: to get an impression of her, and I got one. If that's not enough for unuh to make the right decision then me a go take it outta unuh hand. If both a unuh want fi behave like children, I'll treat unuh like them. I have my impression and the decision has been made: me a take Irie back inna the morning.'

Makeda shoulder sag, but she nah say nothing. 'How can yuh say that after yuh gone and met them?' I say in her place. 'Yuh nah see what kinda people them is, Joyce? Yuh can't engage yuh brain and imagine what kinda life Irie is gonna have with them? Yuh mad?'

'Mrs Roskilly seem intelligent.'

'She never look *that* intelligent.'

'She invite me inside after we talk on her doorstep. She bring me inside her living room where she have nuff book, come like she have every book ever publish.' Joyce was speaking to I&I with her back turn – she'd fetch a stool and was sat in front of a deep-bowl plant, her hand inna the soil. 'She an intellectual type – yuh can tell she actually read the books she own, them weren't just for show. She ax if me want fi borrow a couple, but me never want take nothing from her so we sat and spoke bout how me want fi help and what them do so far, where them look, the authority them contact. She tell me that them inform social service and that the police were beginning an investigation. Me get the feeling she did want someone to speak to, yuh know; some company while her husband was out. She was close to tears when she was telling me bout the likkle girl. I ax her how she found it: raising a black child, and clearly she had given it thought. She a Christian woman, Jabari. She had pure Bible pon her bookcase. I imagine she go to the church down by the park.'

'Did you ax her why she adopt Irie in the first place? I'm sure there were some white baby she could have,' I said, 'white baby not inna the system.' Makeda was still eating, only responding with facial expressions, but I'd lost I appetite.

'I did, yes.'

'So did she look fi a black yute specifically, or did the city stick her with one?'

'She tell me her and her husband did ax for the yute to be black.'

'Why?'

'Said she sympathise with the issue face by our community, want fi do her part.'

'She must think say she some kinda missionary, rudeboy.'

Joyce was firm with her next words: 'I don't agree with her thinking, but so long as she don't make Irie feel like she should be grateful, it don't matter. I tell her that as well and she did agree – though I'm not sure she'd thought that far ahead herself.'

'Of course she agree, yuh were comfy in her yard talking bout books, offering yuh sympathy, making it easy for her to look yuh inna yuh face and lie. I bet yuh never even confront her properly.'

Joyce wasn't rising to I&I temperature at all. 'Me tell her how some people in our community don't appreciate English people adopting black children, told her matter of fact like that, I never have none of yuh childish aggression when I said it, but it was still something she'd never heard, nor consider.' She drag her stool to the foot of a next basin.

'And what she say?'

'She got a likkle defensive at first, went pink how them do, then she say she under no illusion bout Irie being a black girl. She say she know what kinda background Irie come from. I imagine she has a whole file on Cedella and her family history. City would've made sure she knows exactly what went on in that household. She said for now she and her husband gone prioritise what them think are the more pressing things: Irie feeling safe with them; learning not fi run way; eating structure meals; sleep pattern; shelter. Them want fi give Irie the tool she need fi navigate life, so them try teach her resilience, and she say the conversation bout race and politics and them things there will come later.' The more the conversation drag, the more Joyce voice get all mechanical and uninterested, which further rile I&I. 'She tell me that them a come, but she say Irie won't have a chance to engage in discussion bout wider society if her other needs aren't met. Me tell her me was glad she never think love was enough. And she say that love was almost enough, but she make preparations for the things where she anticipate love would fall short. And that's how most of the conversation went.'

The smell of the yard food was making I mouth water. I never eat nothing since that morning, but on Jah I wouldn't fold. 'Things like what?' I said, all serious.

'Her self-esteem.'

'She get that right. It a fall way short.'

Joyce went inna the kitchen area and fill her kettle. 'Mrs Roskilly say she know she won't be able to replace Irie mama, but she can provide her with everything she need.' I never look no place else but her as she talk. Joyce never return the courtesy, though; she did come back and give her attention to her plant again, watering them with the kettle. Makeda was still eating in silence.

'I bet she tell yuh she have black bredrin,' I say.

'She did.'

'Yuh ever see a black couple adopt a white baby, Joyce?' I ax. 'Makeda, yuh ever see that?' Makeda say she never; she say it

151

quietly though, and she did sneak one look at Joyce before she say it. 'It's not a coincidence, yuh know? Only them man do them things there because only them man think say them can. It a special kind of arrogance, bredrin. If one of we ever adopt a white baby it would be natural, yuh know? We wouldn't go shopping for no white baby like how white people do. And Jah know we would raise a white child better than any white person can raise one of we: we been force fi know them for hundreds of years, iyah. We eat them food, learn them language, attend them school, we know white people better than them know themself.'

'She tell me there's a shortage of black adopter in the system. She ax me if I thought it was better Irie was left in the care system, and from everything I know of it from Angela, it certainly is not.' Her back was to I-man again. She set the kettle down beside her and press a finger into the earth.

I point outside. 'Joyce, if we went round the whole of St Pauls right now we'd find every other yard a raise a yute that isn't them yute by blood. We just don't formalise everything with paper and notice and useless things like that.'

Joyce stop her infernal gardening and finally look pon I-man. I could see she nah have no more patience. I could see her jaw through her cheek with how hard she clench her teeth. 'I advise her that she should think bout moving to St Pauls as Irie get older,' she said, speaking every blasted word slow. 'And she look shock, said she couldn't see any reason to, which was short-sighted, but the point is she is using her head, Jabari, more than a likkle. Irie will have a better chance at life with her than with Cedella – and that's a fact.' She sped up. 'It don't matter if yuh agree or not, yute, because like I said, yuh nah have a say anymore. Irie will spend the night here – Makeda, yuh know yuh welcome to as well – Jabari, yuh can go home to yuh mama. In the morning I'll be taking her back to St Andrews and I'll be taking her alone.'

I stood, rushing the words out. 'What would yuh have done if yuh never rate her then? If yuh went visit the Roskilly them and them was as fuck-up as Cedella?' It was like Makeda was no longer there, like Irie couldn't hear we from upstairs. I never business anyway, it was basically done like Joyce say.

Joyce stood too, and this time she spoke as fast as I did. 'It don't matter what I would've done, yute. I'll tell Mrs Roskilly that me did feel so move by our conversation that me put the word out.' She wave her hand. 'Tell her someone found Irie there a Weston – Lord knows how she did get there – I'll tell her whatever.'

I thought say I had her. 'And what happens when Irie tell them bout Makeda and I?'

'I'll say unuh were part of the search party.'

'Chuh! Yuh really a tell I&I that yuh think say the Roskillys can look after Irie?'

'Yes, that's exactly what I think.'

'She has to be with her own kind,' I plead.

'Yuh think being round other black people is all there is to happiness?'

'It's a good start, least none of our trouble won't be because of no white people.'

Joyce lid was now fully cast from her top, but I was vex too. 'Oh yes,' she say, 'the answer is in Africa. "Look to the black man crown king." No!' She drive a fist into her hand, then she lift her finger up and point them at I head, firing bullets in I face. 'We'll best help people like Irie by staying put: in Canada and England, in America – serving the people whose people went through what we went through. We won't do it by chasing a fantasy. Mrs Roskilly was right. Whatever them may be, we all affi have our basic need met before anything else, before we can make plans and dream. And take a look round yuh, my yute, when yuh a walk to the school bus, when yuh on yuh paper round in the morning. Our needs are far from met down here in St Pauls. It's a parent responsibility to ground them yute and give them roots, to teach them flight – give them hopes and dreams, and what? Yuh think someone can give them yute wings inna place like this? Yuh can't, not with how it is. Ras Levi know that, same as I do, but him and the rest of unuh want fi take the wings unuh have and beat them across the ocean. But what would happen if we all up and left like unuh want to, eh? What becomes of all the Iries of England if we all cut and run? So, in answer to yuh fool question, bredda; yes, I do think Irie stand a better chance of growing wings in St Andrews.'

'And what bout root, mmh? Them a give Irie root, too?'

Joyce tut, more than vex that I never agree with her. 'At the end of the day, it's better for her to be inna well-off, English family, who care bout her wellbeing, than with a woman like Cedella, who don't have the wherewithal to care whether her daughter live or dead. That's the sad fact of the matter and that's the final word. Be more like Makeda and learn yuh lesson, yuh idiot.' She return to her stool, her back to I-man once more.

I turn to I silent friend. 'Makeda, yuh not gonna say nothing, Idrin – or yuh just gonna sit there all deaf and dumb?' I couldn't ignite her. It was her very own adopted mother we was against after all – she only push her fork through her food.

'Joyce make up her mind, Jabari,' she say. 'It would be good to have more time to think things through, but—' She still wouldn't lift her head. 'So it go.'

'Fine,' I say. 'Unuh gwan then, do what unuh think best.' I went and unlock the latch on the front door. 'But when unuh take Irie back to that white woman, in that crassis area, make sure she know that I never want her fi go back. And I hope that when Irie get older and the Roskillys them realise that them nah want her no more, when them kick her out and she go back to the city: I hope yuh do what yuh should've done when Cedella ax yuh the first time, Joyce.'

I slam the door as I left and went out into the night, and I&I vexation continue all the way up Frontline, past the bank, where I did arm I-self with a missile and cast it through one of the high window. Glass glitter and fell, the alarm bells did sing, a drunk woman laugh and clap, and I went back to Miss Nefertari house follow by the woman babbling insistence that the real Jesus was a Roman-killing, freedom-fighting Hebrew – and there wasn't no such thing as a peaceful revolution.

10

I went to Mr Delbert at the newsagent inna the morning. The man was a trilby-wearing local icon, deep in him eighties, and him stay inna pinstripe suit. You could call on him at four o'clock in the morning and him would never answer the door till him had change into one of him double-breast. Him mostly speak with him facial expression, and was well-known (and often resented) for having favourite. And in all of St Pauls him most favourite was Miss Nefertari. If ever Miss Nefertari miss the market, you could count on Mr Delbert saving her a couple of him best produce and bringing them to I&I door in the afternoon or evening. Him would never knock, him would wait until somebody else did, or him would sit pon our wall, watching the road, waiting until him was notice. Him would never stay fi talk. Him shut down every conversation with a wave of him hand or a tip of him hat. Nor would him accept Miss Nefertari money – him only hand her him blue-and-white carrier bag full of greens and then him was gone. Ras Levi would tease Miss Nefertari when him come home and see the bag. Him would say she had herself an admirer, and she laugh, safe in the regularity of them joke, and Ras Levi would smile and shake him locs and call Mr Delbert a sweet-boy – call him soft, but I thought gentle was a better word; there was a certain hardiness to it, I thought, and I'd always seen Mr Delbert as strong.

Mr Delbert take I-man inna the back where him keep him papers neatly press and bundle, but before I could take them and start I round, him did have I sit and him went upstairs fi fry I&I some plantain and onions and egg. We eat together, him lean up against the wall, I&I sat at the table, atop a stack of papers. 'Yuh speak to yuh fada?' him ax. I shook I head. Him nah speak for another few minutes. 'Me hear the older yutes from the Gardens talk when them come inna the shop; something a go kick off in the next couple days. Me nah want yuh out when it come, yuh hear?' I nod; it seem as though everybody was talking bout the coming trouble that morning. On the walk to the shop, I overheard some people talking bout a footrace between a copper and a couple rude-boys through the Gardens. The yute them did escape, but apparently the copper had seen one of them with a gun and was offering a sizeable reward for any information. And news had gotten round that somebody vandalise the bank; and I'd even found Miss Nefertari on the phone talking to woman she hadn't spoke to in years. 'All right then,' Mr Delbert say, 'the papers below yuh, I put the bike out front already – yuh know the drill.'

Him went to read at him register. I finish I&I food, wrap up warm, and left. The pushbike out front was older than I was. It had a basket and a round light that lit the road. I put the papers them in the basket and set off. I always avoid going through the Gardens with the bike, so I pull up at the estate edge and paid one of the yutes twenty pence to deliver them instead. I pass the Dug-Out Club and the Bamboo and the Romeo and Juliet where the man were still outside drinking Stripe from the night before. The clubs never want no paper – them host the Day-by-Days – but round the corner was the Orange Grove and them did like to keep up with the time. I went past the adventure playground, and past the Pentecostal church with the broken sign, which them had been collecting to fix for years. After an hour I came full circle, to the Cultural and Community Centre, and I never dash the paper at the centre step. I rest the bike pon its stand, and place the paper neat. I'd learn I&I lesson after the first time I dash it and Ras Levi beat I-man bad.

Once I'd finish City Road, I cycle down along Campbell Street – which was always I last stop – I drop the local bulletin through Miss Nefertari door, then I went back to the news-agent and return Mr Delbert bike. It was bright out by then. The streets were a likkle busier, and somewhere loud music was coming from an open window. It was then, when I was leaving the shop, that I saw Joyce marching down Frontline. She was coming from Campbell Street, and she was furious.

'Jabari!' she bawl out I name when she saw I. 'Jabari, come here.' She point at her feet but continue toward the spot to which I was so suddenly rooted.

'Wagwan?' I said, and I never mean to sound shook but

I could hear the wobble in I voice. 'Yuh take Irie back already?'
Her hand snake out and grab I arm, she clout I behind the ear.
'Ow, Joyce man. Why yuh do that for?'

'Where she there?'

'Who?' I check the road to see if anyone was there to wit-
ness I embarrassment.

'Irie.'

'I don't know. I don't have her!'

'Yuh speak to Makeda?'

'Not since I left the café last night. Joyce, let go, man.'

I try to drag I&I arm back but she only squeeze it harder.
'Yuh sure, yute?'

'I'm sure. What I look like? A magician? Look inna I pocket
if yuh want.'

'Yuh don't know where Makeda is?'

'I don't, man.'

'Chuh.' She let go. 'Makeda take Irie.'

'How yuh mean, she take her? She not in the café?'

'She took her.'

'Where?'

'Yuh think I'd be axing yuh if I knew?' She lick her lips.
'Listen, yute, I'm gonna be down at Talia the whole day now –
her mama pass and there's a Nine Night so I affi be there, yuh
understand. I'll have people looking for Makeda myself, but if
yuh hear anything, or she come find you, then come straight
to Talia, yuh understand what me a tell yuh?'

'Yeah, man.'

'This is not a life lesson no more, Jabari; I told unuh last night the coppers them a investigate, and if them catch Makeda with Irie, them will throw the book at her, yuh understand?'

I did nod, grateful that nobody hadn't seen the big woman bad I-man up in the miggle of the street. 'Overs,' I said, eager to bring the conversation to an end.

'Jabari.'

'I hear yuh, Joyce, man, for real. I'll look for her as well. I'll tell her.'

'Yuh understand it's over now, yeah? If Makeda come looking for help, it's over.' She wait for an answer, but I hesitate, thinking she wasn't finish. 'Jabari, I swear—'

'I overstand, Joyce man. The thing done. It done.'

Joyce exhale. 'Unuh close enough to adult now. Unuh West Indian and from St Pauls; them won't try unuh as children them will do it as if unuh adult, so yuh can either listen to what me a tell yuh, and tell Makeda to take Irie back to St Andrews when yuh see her, or unuh can do as unuh please and face the music yuhself. Either way, me promise, if Irie is not home soon, somebody a go prison with Angela and yuh daddy – and them will go for a long time as well. Remember that.' She went to leave.

'Wait, Joyce.' I gather some strength in I voice. 'If yuh hear back from Makeda before I do, yuh come and let I&I know, all right? That's the deal.'

A smile touch Joyce mouth, 'All right,' she say, and there was something in the way she said it that made I face hot. Soon as she was gone I went back and borrow Mr Delbert bike, and ride straight to Ras Levi allotment, but no one hadn't been there. I went to St Andrews, then down the hill through Easton. I spent the morning and entire afternoon looking, but nothing; Makeda was gone.

By time I got back to St Pauls, school was out, so I rode it into the Gardens and carry the bike to the second floor of the maisonettes. Some part of I-man had already given up hope of finding Makeda, but I had a final place to search. I couldn't remember which flat was Friday flat, so I knock pon any old door and was soon point inna the right direction. Prince open up, frowning – him did see I-man through the peephole.

'What you doing here?' him say, all suspicious.

'Makeda with you?'

'Why would Makeda be with me?'

'Yuh go a school today?'

'Obviously.'

I look past him, down the length of him hallway. 'Makeda at school with yuh?'

'I didn't see her, I assumed she was with you.'

'You never see her or Irie on the bus back neither?'

'No. What's going on?'

I kiss I teeth. 'Yuh sure she not in there with yuh?'

Prince lean out and check the maisonette corridor. 'I'm sure,' him say, but still I never believe him so I did push inside. The flat was small, like the rest of them inna the Gardens, and there was likkle of much significance. There was a stand in the corridor with a telephone, notepad and pen. An embroidered stool was tuck overneath for long conversation. In the kitchen area was a stove, a countertop, a table. It had no wall separating it from the living room, open-plan was how the city would describe it – shit seem an apter title. In the living room was a sofa, a record player – I never recognise none of the record – a television and a heater. The sofa was upholster in velour with its back and arms cover with a couple antimacassar. It face a meter television where one did affi punch coin inna the back. Where most people I knew did long upgrade to electric fireplace and heater with the fleur-de-lis emboss inna the metalwork, like the one Miss Nefertari did have, them still did have an old-fashion heater squatting in the living area. It burnt hot and did produce an acrid smell, which linger pon clothes like old woman perfume. At school Prince tell Cynthia Hughes that Friday call the ancient machine Marcia – because she had the fire of a West Indian in her belly – and every week Prince would affi go a the petrol station and buy a gallon of paraffin fi fill her up. Marcia was the only woman in the flat, neither Makeda nor Irie were there. I kiss I teeth and felt Prince watching I neck from the living-room doorway.

'You believe me now? Took you barging into my house, but you see I was telling the truth now, eh,' Prince said. 'Why would Makeda even be here, anyway?'

'She take Irie somewhere and go missing,' I said.

'She didn't tell you where she went?' Him sound concern.

'Obviously not,' I say, cold as you like.

'Does Joyce not know?'

'No.'

'Her mum?'

'Her mum don't never know nothing bout nothing, rudeboy.'

163

'Why would you think she came here, then?' Him was stuck on that.

'I don't know. Unuh chat init.' I stay by the dining table, him did stay by the door. Him reach inna him pocket and put a pick in him mouth. Him never chew it though, him just leave it there like a farmer piece of hay in American movie, and I did wonder what him would've done in the same situation; whether him would've fought the pigs in order fi protect Makeda, or whether him would've lain there and bawled.

Him walk I-man back through him daddy flat and out onto the corridor where Mr Delbert bike was waiting – I hadn't plan on leaving it long. Prince follow I out. We look out over the playground: the yutes driving the abandon saloon, those sat pon it roof, and the boys still sharing the copper helmet between them. 'How did yuh and Makeda even become cool?' I ax. 'I never even know say unuh know each other till yesterday.'

Prince lean up pon him doorframe and start whorling him pick round him mouth. 'We don't really, I just ax her out before.'

'Wait, yu— yuh did what?'

Him sort of smile, 'She didn't tell you?'

'Nah, she never tell I-man nothing.' I sat on the pushbike seat and held the back brake, rocking the thing back and forth. I never like how happy it make him, standing there so.

'When she said no, I asked her not to tell anyone, but I thought she would've.'

'Makeda wouldn't break no promise,' I said. I gave pause

164

as well, hoping him would continue the story unprompted, but when I glance at him, him still had this bored look about him like him was still waiting for I&I to leave. 'What she say?' I said, swallowing I pride.

'To who?'

'To yuh, when yuh did ax her?'

'She said no obviously, otherwise we'd be going together, that's what people do when one person asks them out and the other says yes.'

'How come she say no?'

Him eye dim. 'I don't know.'

'How she say it?'

'She said it like, *no*.' Prince squint after I-man. 'Why?'

'I'm just axing.'

'I don't know, I guess I don't do it for her. Look—' Two boys and tree girls were scrapping in the playground: the girls were winning, one had a boy by him afro and was beating him with her mama bag, the other two were holding him bredrin back and him was fighting tears. Tree adults, two man and one woman, hurry from them respective yard and from some place outta sight, an elder did call for them to stop behaving like animal. The adults grab each of the yutes by them wrist and frogmarch them inna the same yard, no doubt to lecture and force them into being bredrins once again. I look back to Prince, who was still watching the fallout.

I realise I hadn't really ever seen him hanging round with no one; inside or outside of school, not inna meaningful way, at least; him never have no real pardies like that. I figure him probably sat in him yard all day watching over the Gardens and tending Marcia, doing him homework. I had a vision of him becoming an elder like Battersby and Mr Henry. Him was already the type fi lecture, so him wasn't too far off.

I would've hated having a papa like Friday, I swear. It would've felt like everybody in the community knew I&I most personal business – though, everybody knew I-man business too, cos everybody knew Ras Levi, but it was different. The community respect I papa. Whereas most of them did look down pon Friday – at least the Rases did anyway. And it seem say Prince did as well. Still shuffling on the bike, I glance pon him again. Everybody had something behind them eye. Some had life, like Makeda and Ras Levi; some were angry, like the rudeboy with the snub nose or Miss Francis. I'd always thought Prince did carry a special kind of arrogance behind him eye, same as him papa, one that spoke to him eternal belief in him superiority, but now I kind of thought them look more lonely than anything. Him did watch the yutesdem as though him did know say him miss out on what them have. I follow him line of sight back to the yard what the yutes had disappear inside. Them really were lucky though. Them weren't like Irie, who never have no one, and them weren't like Prince or I neither, who were well use to coming home and not finding no papa.

I let I voice become soft and held out a commiserative olive branch. 'She probably say no because she hear bout yuh axing a load of other girls out, bredda. She not the type of girl who'd go for that, yuh know?'

'What?' Him head jerk toward I. 'I haven't asked anyone out except her.'

'Yeah yuh have.' I frown, not wanting him to take offence, but thinking it common knowledge.

'I would know, wouldn't I?'

'I heard yuh done ax out most of the girls in the Gardens; yuh tell them yuh can take them back to Ghana, no?'

'Who said I said that? Denton?' Him was getting more wound up than I'd intended; him mistake the branch as a whip. 'I've never said nothing like that. I can't take anyone back to Ghana till I get my degree anyway, so whoever said that's definitely lying. The only girl I've ever asked out is Makeda.'

I sat with this for a moment, nodding. I thought him might've ax I-man to leave given the quiet, but him never, and since I never have no place else to go but looking for Joyce there a Talia yard, I further succumb to I curiosity. 'Why yuh ax her specifically?'

'Cos I like her, why does any guy ask a girl out?' Him eyebrows were knit. Him voice all defensive.

'What yuh like bout her?'

'That's a weird question; what do *you* like about her?'

I bunch up I&I face. 'I don't.'

'I mean as a friend, what do you like about her as a friend?'

I felt hot. 'I nah know . . . I guess I like how she talk.'

'How she talks?'

'Yeah, Makeda don't sit on the fence. She happy to be wrong and strong.'

Prince made a face. 'That's the only thing you like?'

167

'Nah, obviously, there are other things too.' I was scrambling. 'That's just the first thing that came to mind.'

'You don't like the way how she smiles?' him ax, glad not to be on the back-foot anymore. 'Or what about her accent? That's probably normal to you though, the Jamaican thing, but I like that. She doesn't come school a lot, but when she does she's actually one of the smartest girls there as well. And, I don't know, you can actually have a proper conversation with her, you know?'

'Yeah, I like that as well.'

Him yawn. 'Well, I like that too, but not as a friend, you know.' Prince tuck one foot overneath the other and fold him arm. 'You know, part of me figured she said no because of you. Since you guys are always hanging out together, I figured she want to still go around with you so she turn me down. Maybe that wasn't all of it. Maybe she didn't like my face; that could be it, but I'm still sure you were a part of her saying no, somehow.'

Immediately, I look down pon the bike and began picking at the rubber round the bike handle. 'She don't like I-man like that, man.' I was speaking fast, too fast. 'If she did like I&I like that, she wouldn't've taken Irie without telling I, would she?'

'I don't know, maybe you're right. I guess the people who like each other spend every chance they can with each other: I haven't ever seen that, though.'

I found more rubber to pick. 'I haven't neither.'

Prince shrug himself from the door and did suddenly become a whole lot more intense. 'Are you waiting for her to say something? Do you like her as well?'

'Nah. I told yuh already, man, I don't like her like that.' I was flush. 'I'm gone anyway, let I-man know if Makeda come back; I'll either be at Talia or Miss Nefertari yard.' I turn the bike in the corridor and him step back inna him hallway. 'Wait,' I call, and him stop. 'Yuh think someone can have a family and commit to the cause?'

'What cause?'

I should've known him never would've get what 'the cause' meant. 'Black power cause,' I say.

'Yeah, why not?' I could tell him never care either way.

I wasn't even sure why I was axing him so important a question, but I was committed. 'Joyce said people affi choose between one or the other: that them can't fit both in them life without making one a them suffer.'

'Your papa does it, though?'

I heart stop. 'Yeah,' I said after a short while, scared that Prince straightaway knew the real reason for I question, wondering if him had some kinda ancient Ghanaian wisdom that could see through I disguise. Clear as day, I heard the voice outside Miss Wilson burning yard saying Ras Levi love himself too much. I heard the voice question him love for I&I. I search Prince face.

'Yeah, so Joyce is wrong then,' him say, still nonchalant, and I knew then that he was still just a yute, him never have no special power.

After another fragile moment I nod goodbye and went to push the bike down the landing, but this time Prince stop the wheel with the bottom of him foot. 'You should make up

169

your mind whether or not you like Makeda you know, Jabari, because the next time I'm with her I'm going to ask her out again, and if you haven't said anything by then, I've got a feeling she'll say yes this time.' Toe to toe we were; him taller in him daddy yard, I shorter on Mr Delbert bike. I stood so we were head to head.

'Get yuh blasted foot off the bike, yuh dutty jankrow yuh,' I said, and I swear I don't know why it drew I-man out so fast, but by time I did ride to the wake at Talia yard, I was still vex.

Talia live inna ground flat next to the Bamboo Club, so it wasn't long after I left Prince yard that I-man was knocking on her front window. It was the evening then. Music thump from inside – no neighbour would be sleeping tonight. Day-by-Days, such as the boy Prince, never did play the rootsy reggae like how we did. Them did play a water-down reggae. The feel-good reggae that the liarsment push in order to dilute the greater Rastafarl message. Them listen to the Tuff Gong that say, 'Herb for my wine. Honey for my strong drink. I shake it easy. Skanky, take it easy.' Them never listen to the Tuff Gong that said, 'Cause the children wanna come home. Africa unite: Cause we're moving right outta Babylon.'

A Day-by-Day whose face I knew, but whose name was foreign, open the door, and as I had expect the house was ram, mostly with pure woman, same way it always was whenever someone pass. I find Talia and give her I condolence – I never know her mama but for wearing fascinators on Sundays and politely bobbing I head at her in the street, but still I call her a nice lady when remembering her with Talia.

The whole of St Pauls like Talia because she was eternally bright. She had pure happiness behind her eye, and even I could admit that as far as Day-by-Days went she was all right. She ran a man barbershop from her living room and bought the yutesdem popsicle inna the summertime. She wrap I inna great hug and sincerely thank I for coming. I ax her where Joyce were there and she send I-man inna the garden. I knew most of the face inna the yard, those I never knew I assume were Talia family from outta town. I heard a few raw accent and figure family had flown in from Jamaica as well. I move through the yard, wagwan-ing people, none of whom were dress in black, and cutting exchange short like only someone who had watch Miss Nefertari could.

As I went through the kitchen I caught a conversation between a leather-jacket rudeboy from the Gardens and a black punk girl, who were huddle tightly beside the back door. It was meant to be hush, but the sound system was nearby, forcing them to shout:

Rudeboy: Them punch her up?

Punk: Mash her up something bad, boy.

Rudeboy: How yuh know?

Punk: My boyfriend's half-sister's dad is a copper. He told her, who told him, and then he came and told me, that he saw two pigs carrying her out from the cell.

The rudeboy recoil.

Rudeboy: Knock out?

The punk nod. She gesture for him to return closer to her mouth.

Punk: A couple of my people are going down to the station tomorrow. You should bring your lot.

Rudeboy: Tomorrow?

Punk: Tomorrow afternoon, yeah.

Rudeboy: Joyce know?

The punk shook her head.

Punk: If you come, are your lot gonna tool up?

I did step outside before I hear the answer. The garden was less ram than inside, but it was busy still. It wasn't as big or as fancy as the one I'd climb into in St Andrews, but it had obviously been look after by somebody who know what them a do – somebody who care. I couldn't imagine Talia tending it, she never seem fi have the patience, so I imagine her late mama did wander over a couple times a week and see to the plant herb and flower and the algae pond that sat inna iron container. It was longer than Miss Nefertari back yard. It had a small patio, which became a pathway that did meander from the back door to the back wall. On the other side of the wall were the gardens of the parallel road. I found Joyce sat with her chair back onto the wall, furthest away from the diluted sound – not that she was oppose to them. She was lounge inna foldable garden chair, feet on an coolbox, bokkle in her hand, and to I surprise, beside her was Friday. 'What yuh a do with him?' I ax as I arrive, cutting them laughter short.

Friday open him arm. Him was drunk. 'Can two friends not sit together and mourn another friend's mother? I like Talia very much, and I liked her mother too, though I admit we never did drink together.' Him and Joyce laugh inna manner that tell I that the closest thing to alcohol that Talia mama ever drank was the grape juice in communion.

'Unuh bredrin?'

Joyce was a likkle drunk too. 'Sometimes,' she said, 'when him not hounding me or trying to steal my one other bredrin from me, getting up to wickedness with her.' The pair laugh again and swat them hand at one another across them garden chair. 'Sit down, Jabari. Come.' She took her feet from the coolbox.

I remain standing. 'I couldn't find Makeda,' I said. 'I check everywhere, cept her daddy yard. I never go down them side.'

'Don't worry yuh head – couple of my people went down to Enoch yard anyway,' Joyce says. 'Him wouldn't let them inside, but them nah see anything to suggest she was there.' She lift her bokkle to her lips. 'Makeda in the wind, but me already wash my hand of the whole thing, anyway. Wash my hand of all West Indian fi the night. Tonight I'm drinking with my African bredrin.'

'Too right,' Friday echo, and him raise him bokkle. 'Let the children raise themselves, I say, same as we did: it's tradition.'

'Do you even know who we're talking bout?' I said.

'Makeda, one would assume,' him say, and I glance at Joyce, who was glaring at I-man from over her bokkle top; she never told him the truth bout Irie. I brush her concern aside. It wasn't like I was going to tell him, anyway. I was only checking that she never had.

'All right. If that's the case then I'm gone then,' I said.

'No stay, stay.' Friday sit up erect. 'Ras Levi and I have never had the chance to talk – your papa is a busy man – so in his place let us tell stories and pick one another's brains while we have the chance. Come, sit, sit. Look where you are. Can't you see that life is short? Sit. Besides, if there's anywhere Makeda is gonna show, it's here.'

I did consider going home, but it was only Miss Nefertari there, and we wouldn't speak. And this *was* where Makeda would show. I took the cooler as I chair. 'You want a stout, eh?' Friday ax. 'There's a few in the box beneath you.' I shook I head; I&I locs did twitch. Him gesture to I hair, ever amuse. 'Oh yes, of course.'

No one spoke for a moment, initially uncomfortable in the unfamiliarity of one another company, then Friday did fold one leg over the other and rest him neckback pon the chair. 'So, Jabari,' him say, 'now that we're here together, you can tell me why it is you don't like me?' Him reach down beside him and drink from him bokkle.

'Why I don't like yuh?' I said, watching as two people pass and greet at Joyce, who greet them back. It was dry, but was getting colder, so more people were returning inside. 'Cos yuh a Day-by-Day. Don't matter if yuh from Africa. It's how yuh move when yuh here – inna England.'

'A Day-by-Day,' Friday repeat. 'And what is a Day-by-Day to the layman?' I explain and him laugh heartily. 'That's good,' him say, once done. 'Yes, I like that, that's good. I think I might use it. Did you come up with it?' There were lights in him eye.

'It him daddy language,' Joyce said. 'Levi was calling people that back when I was in the centre.'

'Of course.' Friday smile. 'But I have words to describe you and your daddy too, you know?' him said. 'I call you delusional, idealist, dreamers.'

I stay very still. 'Call us what yuh want,' I said.

'Leave the boy alone, Friday,' Joyce said.

'You want to know why I call you those names?' Friday scoot forward. We were alone in the backyard now. 'It's because you call Africa "home", and I . . . I don't exactly know why, but it rubs me the wrong way, "home". That's why I call you idealist, delusional dreamers. I posit this: the Rastafarian is a fool.' Friday cross and re-cross him leg. 'Ethiopia is not even your ancestral home. It's Ethiopia you plan to return to, isn't it? Shashamaneland, right? The land promised to you by Haile Selassie? Right? But why not Cameroon, eh? Or Togo? Benin? Or even Ghana? Somewhere you actually have a chance of being from. That would be a stronger point of view to me.'

Him sit back in him chair, drank, then came forward again with another thought. 'What you don't understand, is that the problem is not the land, but the people you'll find there. How will you develop a solidarity between West Indians and the Africans who have never known anything other than Africa?' Him gesture at himself like a one pantomimist. 'I listened to the West Indians when I first came here, eh. I listened to you talk about the struggle and I bought into it, believe me. I fought for this liberation you speak of for years – more years than you've been alive perhaps. But I soon realised that this is not America eh. I woke up and realised that, for the most part, life in England is good, no? Better than America, better than back home. Prince's mama didn't agree. She left us and went back to Ghana. Good for her – at least she's from there; she can trace her ancestry there for hundreds of years.'

I observe as Friday did play with the aureate ring pon him finger, shambling them from one to the next, carefully dodging him wedding.

'I concede to the Rastafarian point that West Indians and Africans were once the same. It's true – but now the only thing we have in common is oppression. You West Indians have adopted too many British practices for us to mingle, and it is contemptible. I mean, truly. Joyce would agree, wouldn't you Joyce? West Indians have forgotten what it means to be African, but you will realise this, when you go. Romance can only take you so far.' Him lean back inna him chair, then did come forward once again. 'When America sent those fifteen thousand African-Americans to Liberia, the African population in the hinterland found that they were dealing not with their former countrymen and comrades, their prodigal sons, but rather with Europeans in blackface. And when your people arrived in Ethiopia, those Rastafarians who first answered Haile Selassie's beacon, they were confronted with not only the man's mortality, but his very flawed existence. King of a starving people, feeding his dogs. Ethiopians likened him giving you that land to a biased European monarch giving land to favourable retainers. At its peak Shashamaneland had no more than – what . . . fifty people? It is hardly an example of success. Besides—'

'Joyce,' I said, through I teeth. 'Tell yuh bredrin if him say another word against His Imperial Majesty I'll ruin the Nine Night.'

'Leave it, Friday,' she sigh, and him hold up him palm.

'I'm gone, Joyce. I'm gonna keep looking for Makeda.'

'Yuh look all day, my yute. Leave her. She near enough a woman now,' said Joyce. 'She make her choice and she'll affi live with the consequence. Same as Angela. Same as us all.'

Friday couldn't stay quiet for long. 'I thought I banned the name Angela tonight, Joyce. Tonight we're here for Talia and we're drinking and we're laughing, and we're now in the company of this headstrong young man – even if he keeps trying to leave us.' Him quieten and bring him bokkle to him lip. 'Your Angela will be fine, same as always, eh.'

Joyce readjust in her seat and liquor spill from her glass. 'Not this time. This time she gone where we can't follow, Friday. And this time she'll be gone for a long time too.'

Friday toast the night, and his next words kept I standing there. 'I'll miss drinking with that woman. To me, she is the best of your people, because she understands who she is: a nomad, a sparrow. Her ancestors travelled the passage and were forced to work the land. Now she's answered England's invitation and found that, in fact, the roads are not gold – so, where to next? Just like the nomad, a woman like Angela don't worry bout such a question – it isn't a question that should incite fear but excitement. She was free. Now the city has seen to clip her wings – though I'm sure there is a certain romance to that as well – and so . . . to a woman who founded her home in the people around her, the people she loved, people, like both Joyce and I, who are blessed to have been in her company . . . to Angela.'

The two a them clink them glass and with the arrival of those who had been outside in the garden with I&I, the music had been turn up inside, and the tree of we all turn when the bass of one of Dennis Brown big tune kick in.

11

I left Talia yard not long afterward. The spring evening was gloomy and I could hear raise voice in the distance – nothing unordinary, but as soon as I reach Frontline I was accosted. 'Jabari!' come the voice across the street, but rather than respond, I quicken I step, not in the mood, thinking about Makeda, and what Friday said, and trying to outrun them. 'Jabari!' the voice come again – this time I recognise it as Denton.

'Wahum?' I said, and I did see him was with two next Rasta boys who'd stop some way ahead of him and were shouting for him to hurry.

'The centre,' Denton say. Overneath him, him feet shuffle toward him companion. One of him hand was cover in bandage. Him point it toward City Road. 'The coppers them raid it.' Together we took off, and we found at least twenty pigs outside the centre, the blue lights of them panda car flashing, lighting the dark, and if everyone wasn't already in the street or hanging from them window, them would've woken them. 'Yo Jabari, I'm sorry what happen to yuh pops, man,' Denton say, as we push through the crowds of people. 'I never had the chance to tell yuh this time.'

I nod I head slightly in acknowledgement.

Him did have more to say. 'Before we leave England, I swear we should burn the police station like how Angela was gonna burn the bank.' Then a pause. 'Yuh think the coppers think we had something to do with Angela?'

'Maybe.' I shrug. I soon lost him and the two boys amongst the crowd: there was almost as many as had been in the Gardens, and the road was getting busier as the watchers from the windows made them way downstairs. I heard a voice calling for the coppers them fi fuck off, and Miss Francis had found another pulpit from which to preach. Ras Joseph and another Ras were keeping Sister Dorothy in somebody front yard, trying to stop her from attacking the coppers. Ras Stephen was stood to another side of the road; the copper never trouble him shoe this time. Him touch him heart and did hold up him hand when him see I-man; I held up mine.

When I arrive at the foot of the centre, the pigs were already streaming out, so I bound up the step, ran through the shatter door and inna the lobby where Bandulu was barking order. The coppers had been in the kitchens. Everything in the cupboard and the fridge and the bins was on the floor, all the couscous and the dry fruit and the beans and the pulses had been open, and all the fruit and vegetable had been crush underfoot. The workshop and the classroom were the same: all mash up and turn over, the chair and table were upside down and there was a crack inna the window. The radio station was the same: the pigs had rip the mic from them plug-in and the mixing console from the wall. The centre had been raid before, nuff time, but this was the worst I'd seen it. It seem we were destine to be nomad after all – Friday wasn't wholly wrong. I took to the stairs in disbelief, and found that them had been to the fourth floor as well.

It was then I did remember the pardna. I'd heard plenty a story bout pigs arresting people and taking the coin from them pocket, and note from overneath them mattresses, and never was the money seen again. I went inside for the first time in I life. It wasn't anything special: a meeting room with a round table and desk. There was a small toilet and sink in the corner, no bigger than a cupboard. The sink was crack and water dribble from the pipe. Somebody had put a bucket overneath to collect it but the bucket was nearly full. I open the window and toss the contents onto the street. I slam the window shut and threw the bucket across the room where the plastic shatter against the wall. If the pigs had taken the pardna there would be no getting it back: we were stuck here. Against hope, I search the ceiling, and the bathroom, I press pon walls hoping one would spring aside and reveal a secret compartment or something, but it was all in vain.

Outside, the streets were the same as I did leave them – except the coppers had wisely made a swift exit.

Ras Joseph caught I inna miggle of the street. Him tell I that Ras Levi was home: in Miss Nefertari house. Him tell I to look after him when I seen him, but before him could finish giving him instruction, I had already began fi run, and I never stop until I was on the other side of Miss Nefertari door.

I could hear Ras Levi in the kitchen with Miss Nefertari, Gil Scott Heron 'We Almost Lost Detroit' on the record player, I parents voices too low to catch: I could still hear the tumult outside as well, it seem no one was interested in going home. Miss Nefertari call I name from the kitchen, and I kick off I shoe. 'Papa here?' I call back. Miss Nefertari ax if I was alone. She explain that she was force fi turn way a million well-wishers as I walk through to the kitchen, and when I arrive I saw the reason why: Miss Nefertari was stood, seeing to the wounds of a seated, shaven-head man, with cotton wool and rubbing alcohol. The man hair was no longer wild or manly: it was gone. The man was loc-less.

Him lift him terrible head. 'Come sit, Jabari,' Ras Levi say, but still I never move. On the short run here, I had already steel myself in preparation of finding him with puffy lip and open cut; to find him usual good posture lopsided, with him shiny eye rebellious in them broken socket. I'd seen that story plenty of time, and it was as much the case now as it had been as then, but I never expect this. I went to ax him whether him was all right, but with the way him look, I held I tongue, swallow, never mention nothing bout nothing at all. 'Son,' Ras Levi eventually said – him voice as strong as ever. 'Come sit down, and make I&I speak as fada and son. Come.' I start, and did as I was told, not so much because him ax, but because I was suddenly exhausted. I pull a chair from the dining table and sat opposite him. 'Greet your mama,' him say.

'Good evening,' I said, without moving.

'Jabari.'

'Good evening, Miss.'

Him stroke him head from front to back. Him look age. Him make a short sound. 'Yuh shock right? Beastman come inna I cell when I was sleep, Jabari, took five a them man fi pin I-man down and cut I&I pride.' Him wave him hand cross the kitchen. 'Locs strewn across the floor like hay inna barn ready fi blow through the window in the wind.' Him grunt again. 'By time them finish I still had the odd piece of hair growing from I head, looking a mad fool, Jabari. I did affi swallow RastafarI pride and ax them for a razor to finish the job.' Him pause. 'Coppers hurt yuh after them took I away?'

'No, sir.'

'Them hurt anybody else?' The doorbell rang and Miss Nefertari left to answer it. I heard her telling whoever it was that Ras Levi wasn't accepting no visitor.

'Them hit a couple people, sir.'

'That it?'

I bit I lip. I wasn't going to tell him bout St Andrews or Irie, not now. 'Mostly, them just run off with yuh and Angela. It's been quiet since then, nothing much happen, no.'

'Quiet?'

'Mostly; though I heard some people talking bout doing something in retaliation.'

'Mmmh, that's what I been hearing as well,' him say, and when Miss Nefertari return, she dab her cotton wool and apply fresh alcohol and I saw I papa wince. 'I heard even the

183

Day-by-Days want fight back this time,' him say, and him laugh. 'I don't buy it for a second. What make this time different from the last hundred time? Them can't be doing it for I-man sake.'

It was quiet for a bit after that, as we each sat with our thoughts and the noise outside. Ras Levi hum to Gil Scott, but unusually for him, him was well outta time. Gil Scott went one way and Ras Levi went another; singing a separate song, with another melody. 'Yuh know, Jabari, when the pig hit yuh . . . I just see red, yuh know? That's something I-man pass to yuh: yuh temper. That's something him get from him daddy, isn't it, Miss Nefertari?' Miss Nefertari confirm that it was. 'Most of the time it's a curse; having a temper like fi we temper, but one thing it good for is protecting people.'

Him reach forward and pat I&I knee with him rough, sander hand. It was strange. The whole thing was strange, but I knew I couldn't leave. 'I'm glad yuh well, yute, better them dash I-man inna cell and cut I hair than you. Better that.' Him show I-man him knuckle. Them was sharp and tall pon him hand. I thought a man jaw might shatter if him did tump them, and them was damage, same as mine. 'All these years and I still haven't work out how to properly channel I anger, iyah, but I've been better, isn't it, Miss Nefertari? Yuh mama can tell yuh what I was like as a boy in Jamaica, she left and came here before I did. I swear I was mad, Jabari, fighting every day, running up inside people houses who mad I, nobody couldn't tame I; I was a lion. That side of I-man still hasn't gone, no matter how many years of peace and love go by, it don't go, but like I said, it's that side what hold the community together, you know?' The doorbell went again and again, Miss Nefertari went to answer. Ras Levi eye turn glass like Makeda in St Andrews.

'I've given everything to St Pauls, Jabari. Everything I've ever had I did, I gift-wrap and hand it to St Pauls; to the people. I did so because Jah ax I-man to come here to this wicked land and deliver Him message. Every community needs a prophet, but it's tiring work, Jabari. I know yuh seen how I am whenever I come home. I eat whatever Miss Nefertari cook then go straight to bed, and it's cos I'm shattered, iyah. Every day I go to the centre and give it everything. There from morning to noon to night, making sure the people them eat and the yutesdem have them creche, sorting out adults squabbling with one another like children, making sure the drummers have fi them rhythm, the chanters know them chant, the nursery worker have them toy and chalkboard, and everything tick round like clockwork. All the while reminding people of Jah bigger plan: of the final goal of repatriation and returning home to the fatherland, cos everybody need a home. Yuh know the thing already.' Him wipe him face. 'Boysah, blood, sweat and tears I've given to this place, boy. Built the centre with I own hand. Made it into what it was today: a place where the people can seek refuge from the pigs them; from unemployment, give them something to keep busy with; from discrimination and the evils of capitalism—'

Him stop, and him look past I&I as if a duppy was over I shoulder, but it was only him woman. 'Them forward in

I cell another time, yuh know Jabari,' him say. Him stroke
him beard and lower him voice. Him lean forward and invite
I-man fi do the same. I could feel the heat of the sweat pon him
face. 'Two coppers forward in I cell, and them did ax where
the money was.' Him sit back and laugh, too loud, then him
repeatedly rap I chest with him hand and set I heart beating
nuff. 'So hear what I say, I say: "What money? What money
yuh a talk bout?" Them tell I&I not to play games with them.
Bear in mind; whole time I'm cuff, yuh know bredrin? Whole
time. So I tell them, "What money?" And them box I inna
I face, just like that.' Him flick I face with him sharp knuckle.
'Just like that, and I never do nutun, because I couldn't: I two
hand tie.' Him flick I face again.

'Them say, "The money yuh a use fi go back to Africa."
And I said to I-self, *Bloodclart; them know bout the pardna?* But
out loud I raise up I head and say, "I thought yuh want I&I fi
leave, bredda?" And them say, "Yuh can leave after we take the
money,' them say. "Why don't yuh try swim there instead?"'
Ras Levi slap him knee and laugh again. 'Yuh see how them
funny, Jabari? Yuh see how the white man a joke?' Him stop
laughing. 'Yuh remember I tell yuh the problem with the IRA
is that them enemy favour them, yuh remember? Jah know
say it come back to bite I, because them tell I-man that them
have an informant inna I&I camp. Them say them record him
name simply as RASTA: I wonder how many piece of silver
him went for. How much yuh reckon, yute?' Him sidle closer
and the suddenness of him action made Miss Nefertari spill
rubbing alcohol down him bald head and it fell down him face,

but him left it there, same way, as though him never notice, as though him a bathe in it. 'European tactic never change, Jabari. Them do the same thing on local and national level: disruption and theft, it in them nature.

'I try tell the coppers that them can't raid the centre without a reason, but them say them will find one, say them will connect Angela crime with RastafarI. Them ax I whose side I think the court will take when them go for a warrant.' Him wipe him face again and sigh. 'Them never tell I-man who RASTA was; likewise I wouldn't confirm any knowledge of the pardna neither. Them try exchange the two, but a grass is not enough bargaining power for a man like Ras Levi.' Suddenly him was up, beating him chest and shouting: 'Duppy know who fi frighten!'

Miss Nefertari gave up cleaning the man head. She was near enough done, anyway. Him skull shine it was so clean. The kitchen light bounce from it. Him was naked. I was numb. 'It's hard, finding a balance between a man responsibility as a fada, and him responsibility to Jah. I am responsible for the physical and spiritual wellbeing of I&I people in St Pauls. RastafarI people. Jah people inna this community. It is I responsibility to lead them from this desert, back to Ethiopia, where we might be free of all a Babylon fuckery – excuse I language Miss Nefertari – but that is what it is – fuckery. Since moving to this forsaken land, since Miss Nefertari born yuh, I've sacrifice a relationship with I only son, to do what was right for the people, but now Jah tell I that Him have a new plan for we. Him come inna I cell and tell I-man that Him want we fi go inna new direction.'

187

Ras Levi would often lecture I&I on Jah calling, and whenever him do so, I would see a crown pon him head, bright enough to attract magpie to the sill, but now it was like I never did recognise the man in front of I – this man who crack. Him see the confusion which disturb I feature. 'Jabari.' The room turn dark, frighten by him volatility. 'Yuh overstand everything what I teach yuh, don't yuh?'

'Yes, I think so, sir.'

'All what I teach bout repatriation, returning to our true home?'

Friday word *nomad* was still reverberating in I head. 'Yes, sir,' I said.

'Good.' Him turn. 'Miss Nefertari, leave Jabari with I for a second. Make the lion talk to him cub without the lioness present.' Him slap her backside when she pass and she jump, and him wait until she gone. 'Listen Jabari.' Him rest himself pon I shoulder, him finger clasp round the back of I head. 'I will never put the needs of the people above the needs of this family ever again. I won't ever do it. That's done. From now on it's bout I&I. Of course, the people matter! The people always matter, Jabari, but now it's bout this here family. Yuh overstand?'

'Yes, sir.' I swallow, and I head fell to the floor.

'This is what Jah told I-man, yuh overs?'

'Yes, sir.'

'Yuh like the sound of that?'

'Yes, sir.'

'Then I need yuh to go do something for yuh papa. Come,

188

look at yuh daddy.' I went to lift I head but I was too slow. 'Look at yuh daddy!' him say again, and so I did, and once more him voice quieten. 'I can't go outside, looking the way I do, specially not with the tension how it is in St Pauls right now: the way how I look right now would be the touchpaper that burn this whole place to ash. I need yuh to go and fetch something for yuh papa and bring it back to Miss Nefertari house. Yuh can do that?'

'Yes, sir.'

'Yuh a good boy, Jabari. Yuh a good boy.' Him let go of I head. 'There's a hole overneath a couple of slab at the edge a the Gardens – a gunman use fi keep him weapons there, but him long dead now, I seen him go bury him guns there when I first come a England and I never forget, I never forget.' Then him give I-man the details of where the slab lay. Him go on: 'The pardna inna one bag bury deep where the gunman use fi leave him gun. I want yuh fi go and fetch it and bring it here to Miss Nefertari yard.'

I never overstand.

'When yuh come back we will apportion what is ours,' Ras Levi explain. 'What this family deserve. Then we will be leaving for Shashamaneland tomorrow.' Him walk to one a Miss Nefertari cupboard. 'This is what Jah tell I last night in I cell. We're going home, Jabari. We're not waiting for the sheep no more. Not with this bloodclart informer inna we community.' Him pause, a second away from speaking murder. 'Now is the time for we to go on, Jabari.' Him crouch at Miss Nefertari cupboard and took a mug from inside. 'The longer we stay here, the more we rot, and the closer our souls get to breaking, and I can't be done with all of it no more.'

I was breathless. 'Pa – but what bout your responsibility to the people, Papa? What bout—' Ras Levi walk calmly across the room, open him palm and slap I-man across the mouth.

Him return back to the sink, serene. 'Go upstairs and pack yuh things them, once yuh done go and see bout what I tell yuh fi do.' Him fill the mug with hot water and bring it to the side of him mouth where him lips still had a likkle mobility left, and him drink. The water what miss him mouth spill down him neck and paint him vest. Him catch I staring. I hurry to do as I was bid. 'Yuh always had a soft heart, Jabari.' Ras Levi call after I. I come to a stop on the other side of the kitchen door. Him drain him glass and ran the tap. Him let it run a while, testing it temperature with him wrist. 'What yuh want end up like? Makeda daddy? A man who left him family and end up with a white bitch?' Him was still so calm. 'Yuh want be like him? Cos that's what will happen if yuh carry on talking back and not listening to yuh fada, yuh know? When yuh a argue with yuh papa, know that yuh a argue with Jah, the Almighty-I, remember that, my yute.' And I don't know what him see in I&I face as him speak, because I desperately try to keep any and all emotion subdue. I put a pillow over I-man feeling of defiance and had them die, I kill I every emotion – as I always did do whenever Ras Levi was home – but this time it never work, because him stroke two finger across him bottom lip. 'Matter of fact—' Ras Levi call Miss Nefertari back inna the room, call her normal, like say him was bout to suggest we go fi a fancy. 'Gwan and fetch I the belt,' him say, 'and the bucket from upstairs beside the toilet.'

Miss Nefertari look between we, and I bit I tongue – accepting I fate. 'Levi—'

'Do it,' him say again, and so Miss Nefertari did. She fetch the things them then made herself scarce, same as she always did whenever it came time for a beating. Ras Levi told I-man to go ahead and wait with the belt and bucket in the living room. I went and set the belt pon the plastic arm of the sofa and the bucket in front a it. Then I roll up I trouser leg in preparation. A whole heap of long and short scar did run up and down the length of I two calf. Some was recent and red, some were brown. Then I stood atop the bucket with one-leg. It was better to be ready. Gil promise of revolution kept I-man company, anyway. Ras Levi arrive a few minutes later and took him place on the settee. Thirty minutes pass before I wobble and put a second foot on the bucket. Ras Levi flog I calf with the belt buckle, and from then on, any time I put I foot down, him do the same. After ten minutes I calves were open and there was blood pon the floor.

Ras Levi check the clock on the wall and stood. 'I'm doing what's right for this family, Jabari – what is right by Jah,' him coolly say. 'The way yuh soft is yuh mama fault. Her with her wanting a daughter and treating yuh like yuh was one as a yuteman: keeping yuh hair so pretty so. Miss Nefertari an intelligent woman, but she a woman still, and one day, one day soon Jah-willing, yuh will be a man. I suppose, it I-man fault as well.

I spend so much time outside the yard with this here ungrateful community, but things will be different in Shashamaneland. Things will be different indeed. Come now, get down.'

I stagger from the bucket. Him catch ahold of I arm and kept I upright. Him send I upstairs to bathe and I saw that Miss Nefertari had already pack up the house.

I lower I-self inna the bath and sank until only I nose was above the water line. Again I did turn the water pink, then brown. It stung when I soap I skin but I sat in silence with the pain. Once done, I went to pack I things for Ethiopia, where Miss Nefertari did find I-man stoop over I bag, ready to roll I clothes and stuff them inside. She come inside a the room and shut the door, all quiet like. 'Yuh all right?' she say, her hands behind her back, still on the doorknob.

I never show no emotion. 'Yes, Miss.'

'Him think say yuh would be excited to go, Jabari,' she say. 'That's why him react like that: yuh fada upset yuh never support him.' She pause, but if it was I-man turn to speak, I wasn't going to, so she continue: 'I try tell him yuh too old to hit now, but him never listen.' It went quiet again as I continue to pack. 'Him never know how fi talk to yuh, Jabari – that's what it is. Member him lose him mama young, Jabari, him nah know no better.'

I never turn from the bag. I took a shirt, did fold it arm and roll it. 'Miss Nefertari?' I said, thinking that the night was already so full of surprise and change that it wouldn't feel so wrong to add to it.

'Yes, baby.'

'Yuh think God really tell Papa to go to Shashamaneland right now, without the rest of the RastafarI people?'

Miss Nefertari falter. 'He might've, mightn't He?'

Ras Levi voice travel from him place inna the kitchen and summon him woman. I turn for the first time since Miss Nefertari arrive to find her opening the door with a gentle hand pushing against it, praying the sound of the click never reach downstairs. Not wanting to get her into trouble, I wait until she manage it and kept I voice low.

'Miss?' She stop in the hall, lips apart, listening. 'If Jah ax yuh to take I-man up to the mountain and sacrifice I&I like Him did with Abraham and Isaac, would yuh do it? Would yuh do it if Him ax yuh to?'

Miss Nefertari mouth open and close. 'There's a reason Him ax Abraham and not Sarah,' she say, eventually.

I nod; she was probably right, but still. 'Then how come yuh always leave every time Papa tell yuh to fetch the belt and bucket?' I said, and it wasn't said with any malice, I promise it wasn't; only curiosity, a curiosity that had eaten away at I-man ever since Miss Nefertari and I had stop being close. There was hope there too; a hope that I mama might be able to explain away years of separation and hurt with a single sentence. 'How come we never talk no more?' I say. 'Was it something I did wrong? Because of what happen with Pretty? Because if it was, it wasn't I fault, yuh know Mama, it wasn't.' I was speaking too loud; she shush I-man and check her shoulder.

Ras Levi call for her again. I held her eye until she drop

193

it. I was desperate for her to say something. To feed I-man a line that would make I immediately overstand. One line that I could accept, because I was lost.

'I'm sorry, baby,' she say. 'I affi go . . . see yuh daddy, if him know say we did talk after him already discipline yuh, him will probably think I was undermining him, then him will start talk bout leaving again; yuh know yuh fada.' She smile weakly, then she hurry to the top of the stairs. 'Jabari, yuh affi give it a chance, all right?' she whisper. 'Give yuh papa a chance. For yuh mama . . . please? Can yuh do that?'

'All right,' I said, cold. Miss Nefertari smile, missing her son broken heart.

Soon as I finish packing, I went to the place Ras Levi describe; overneath the archway where the sticksmen hang, the second slab from the left, next to the wall. It never wobble, but after I fit I fingers down the side of the thing, it did come up with a strong tug – just like how Ras Levi say it would. Overneath was a large hole, and in the hole was a boxer bag. I took it out, put the long strap over I shoulder and fix the slab back over the hole. I check say no one never see and hurry away. Ras Levi tell I not to unzip the bag, but I did, and I swear I couldn't fathom the amount of paper money inside, let alone count it. There seem to be hundreds of stacks. I zip it back and got outta the estate as fast as I legs could carry I, except I never travel back to Miss Nefertari yard on Campbell Street. Instead, I went and call pon the Mother Earth.

12

Joyce let I-man in the back and led I through the café. She was in her dressing gown and slippers. She flick the light. Aside from the greenery the room was barren: the metal table and chair had been stack and set aside; the patty inna the oven were gone and there was a bin in the centre of the room – the place smelt of burnt paper. 'Me get rid of everything except the plants and the books,' Joyce explain. 'If them did raid unuh cos of Angela, them will definitely raid the Mother soon; that's my thinking.'

'Makeda nah show at Talia?'

'No, sir.' She turn the light off and beckon for I-man to follow her upstairs; this was the most quiet I'd ever seen her. It was like a whole other woman, really. She seem soft, like how a mother should be. She ax if I want food, a drink, what I was doing out so late. And I did answer all her question politely, turning her down. 'I'm sorry to hear bout the centre, man,' she say. 'I hear them do a real number on it this time. A whole heap of people come Talia yard after; come tell me what happen. Me and Friday went up there as well. I never seen Ras Joseph so vex.'

'I don't know why yuh a apologise for, it wasn't yuh who do it.'

'I told Angela this would happen,' she said, and when we reach her flat, she boil the kettle for tea and I set down in the sofa. I kept the boxer bag between I leg. 'Angela did always hate that there bank,' Joyce say from the kitchen. 'She always go on bout how it was a crime that a bank built with slave money was stood proud in the same neighbourhood as the son and daughter of those same slave.' She brought I tea and sat in an armchair by the window. There was a lamp behind the chair. The window was shuttered with Venetian slats. She turn them clockwise till she could look out pon the racist bank. She drink her drink. 'The last time she go on about it to me was a month back. Angela and Friday usually go out drinking twice a week, but this was them third time. Friday, man.' She shake her head. 'If that man's not giving you headache with how much him go on bout things, then it's the liquor him make yuh drink, and it's never him who wake up with a hangover; the man a rogue. The two of them make sense though, in some ways them good for each other. I couldn't never keep up with how much Angela want to go out, so together them would travel to shubeens all over the country. She drag him to some lecture or some kind of protest in the afternoon, and him would complain, but really, him love argue with activist, and Angela like seeing him get under them skin. Then them would hit the town in the evening. She a party girl, Angela is. I'm more an inside body, yuh know? I like my plants and my books them and my own company, yuh know.'

'She like Makeda – she likes moments.'

'Exactly,' Joyce say. I was glad for her going on, it gave I&I time to think. 'Those two as well, man. Them was alike before them even meet. Them argue all the time, but only because them so similar.' She pull the slats up till the view was free from restriction. 'A month back Angela and Friday went out, same as normal; usually them would both come back to the Mother in the morning – bout four or five. I'm an early riser so I never mind. Them would come and recount the night. Friday would drink some more. I'd make Angela and I tea. Sometimes we'd have music, and the party would continue here until we open for business. This time, even though them had gone out together, only Angela come back. I ax her where Friday was, but she was skittish; she never respond. I could tell she'd had too much to drink, but it don't take much for her to get going, so I never think nothing of it really. She come and roll up the blind—'

'Like how yuh have them now.'

'Mmmh, like how me have them now, and she look out the window and tell me how she was sick of having the bank watch over we. She say she want it gone. I'm far from a pacifist, Jabari, but I tell her not to do it. It wasn't a matter of whether it was possible. It ain't no trouble for people like us getting whatever we need; with the business we're in, we know some serious people, star. But I told her it would bring hell pon St Pauls. We'd be inviting all sorts of madness. Angela nod and agree, tell me I was right and she drop it.' She snort. 'The only thing Cedella say right the other day, was bout Angela and the

197

damn bank, cos that's exactly how it went. She lie in my face and start setting everything in motion the next day. I never know at the time of course, but she did speak to some of our more militant contact. Told them not fi tell me. These are my bredrins we're talking, my bredrins from when first I come here, but Angela can be real convincing when she wants to be.'

Joyce rub her chin against her shoulder; a small comfort, I guess. 'She plan it all behind my back, bredrin, and she was good to go. She have enough explosive to take down the bank and rip a hole in the neighbouring building too.'

'How come the pigs them find out?'

'She and Friday went out drinking to celebrate a couple nights ago, although I'm sure Friday never know what it was them a celebrate. Them get drunk over a game of domino and she start brag bout it – she tell the people them was playing with to withdraw them money from the bank. Then one of them went and snitch to the beastman.' Joyce drank her tea, which must've been cool.

'RASTA.' I nod, speaking mostly to I-self.

'I don't know who she was with,' Joyce say. 'Friday say him nah remember. Him tell me a whole heap of name, but none of them sound like the type to grass. Still, yuh never know. I have my suspicion, but them lucky me can't say for sure.' She drink again and squint at the stars. 'I couldn't bring myself to come down to the Gardens when the coppers took her. I couldn't bear it.' She smile. 'Makeda did, though.'

'Yuh worry bout her?'

'Who, Makeda? Me worry bout them both. Them so similar,

man. It's like Makeda Angela baby, not her mama. Makeda was born not long after I first start up this place. I went round to see her mama when she did born. She was a precious thing. Then the Mother became what it became and Enoch left and Makeda mama turn her back on me completely – them all did – but neither she nor I, really, expect Makeda to grow up and come in the Mother by herself one day.' She laugh like a mischievous likkle girl. 'I can still see Makeda face when she first come in: a frighten likkle thing, but she had some courage still, it take a lot for stranger to step foot inna the Mother. She stood over the man playing Ludi. After she watch a while and she see them gambling, she took out her likkle piece of money and ax them if she could play. I start calling her my daughter bout two months after her first visit. Angela took a likkle longer to warm to her, but that's how she stay: she very protective of me and this place, but I think Makeda taught Angela a lot.'

'Like what?'

'She taught both of us. She don't know it, but she did. Children teach yuh things, Jabari. Them teach yuh that the world is a terrifying place, full of danger. Before Makeda, it was just Angela, but now the two of them are the only people I can say I love more than myself. Yuh have anyone yuh love more than yuhself, Jabari?'

I thought bout it. 'I don't know.'

'Not Ras Levi?'

Ras Levi. Ras Levi. 'I don't know,' I said.

'It's not a matter of knowing, it's more a feeling really. A feeling what show itself in yuh action, then when yuh reflect

pon them yuh realise the truth was there the whole time.' She
fell quiet. 'I can't lose both her and Angela in the same week,'
she say. 'I don't know what fight I'd have left.'

'She'll be all right,' I said, after a moment pass. 'I won't let
nothing else happen to her, and yuh won't, neither – between
I&I we'll keep her safe, man.'

Joyce smile at I-man and return to the night sky. 'City won't
forgive St Pauls for what Angela try do,' she say. 'Watch, them
will punish this area for years to come, punish we till them
ready fi come take it back.'

I unzip the boxer bag and push it toward the armchair with
I foot. I never say what it was. Joyce frown before leaning from
her chair and pulling the two sides of the bag apart. Her eye
widen and she mutter 'rahtid' overneath her breath. She dip
her hand inside and finger the money. She brought two stack
from inside and flick through them, inhaling as she count.
'Ras Levi pardna?'

I nod.

'Rahtid,' she say again.

She ax how I came by it and so I did explain: Ras Levi
appearance, what him ax I-man fi do, how him beat I for
talking back, beat I-man for not supporting him weakness.
I never mean fi tell it all, and still I don't know if I'm proud
that I did, but once I did start I stood up and pace the room,
spoke in a raise voice. The whole while, Joyce sat over the
money, chin resting pon her fist, listening silently, and once
I&I finish she hmmed. 'So what issue yuh have with what Levi
tell yuh, then?'

'What issue?' I said, talking with I hand as much as I mouth. 'Joyce, if I let him leave then him a abandon everything him ever teach I-man. I whole life him teach I-man that it's bout the whole collective RastafarI people. We affi wait for the people. We affi wait for the people. That's why him spend so much time at the centre – fi the people, the people, the people! That's what him always drive home, Joyce: the people. Him say don't waste time thinking bout the I, think bout the I&I, the whole of we as one. Now him a tell I that Jah want him fi turn him back upon the RastafarI people of St Pauls? From a yuteman him tell I this mission him have was given by God, and now him a try abandon it.' I took a breath. 'If I take him back the pardna now, him will divide it up and I&I will be gone in the morning: off following this new plan.'

'And if yuh don't take it back, what?'

I swallow. 'Then him won't never love him son again. Miss Nefertari won't neither, she follow whatever him say.' I voice trail off, till I raise I head. 'What would yuh do, Joyce?'

'That's what yuh come for? To ax me that?'

'I want to see if Makeda was here.'

'To ax her?'

'Yeah.'

'Yuh not a man?'

I teeth grit. 'Don't ax I-man nothing yuh already know, man.'

'So yuh can't make up yuh own mind?' She come forward to the edge of her armchair. Her back straight. Her strong legs wide. 'Yuh ever doubt yuh papa before?'

'Never.'

'So why start now?'

'I done told yuh already,' I say, and this time it was I&I turn to outstretch I arms, 'because it go against everything him ever teach in the past.'

'Well now him a show yuh something new.' I could see her getting as frustrated as I was; it was a bad mix, Joyce and I, we were two hotheads inna small flat. 'Look, if yuh nah want fi take it to him then there is plenty of things yuh can do with that money.'

'Like what?'

She roll her eye. 'Yuh can put it back where yuh find it, take it to Ras Joseph, leave it on some lucky person front doorstep, burn it. Yuh can do anything yuh want with it, yuh have it, don't yuh?'

'What would yuh do with it?'

'Me already tell yuh.'

'No, but what would you do, Joyce? I'm axing you seriously now.'

Joyce could see that I wasn't making no joke, still she remain at the edge of her chair, impassion. 'Well, I would pay some people rent, specially them over in the Gardens. Give them some breathing room. Clear a few people debt. Buy first-aid kit and hire some nurse, like yuh have over the centre, build a rape centre here in the Mother. Then, I don't know, it's a big question, yuh know. I guess I would try buy the place next door so I could extend the Mother, have a bigger library. Look, listen' – she almost tut – 'it don't matter what I would do with it, man. Yuh either need fi follow after yuh papa, same as yuh always done, or yuh need to start to man up and think for yuhself, star. Develop a brain. Make yuh own choice.'

'In yuh plan, would everything be open to RastafarI too?'

'Rasta always welcome in here,' Joyce say. 'It's unuh who nah want fi come.'

I stood. 'So what if I give it to you, then?'

'Yuh think the rest a the Rastafarians won't start a war for what's inside the bag? I can't take it, man. Besides, Levi don't want all the money, no? Him just want a piece.'

'Him say him want what him feel say him owe.'

Joyce nod. 'So if yuh take this money back, yuh'll leave with him and Miss Nefertari in the morning, which is what you've always want, right?'

'Right,' I said, mechanical again.

'And him nah go abandon RastafarI, because him will leave them the rest of the pardna money, probably with Ras Joseph, right?'

'Right.'

Joyce she put her feet up on the coffee table, and instead of the window and the night sky she give her attention to the boxer bag – to the money poking its head from the open mouth. 'Member how we went to Cedella yard and me tell yuh how she let Irie pull the pan from the stove and she bring her round the Mother and had me look after her?' She was stock- still. She never move to scratch an itch, nor did she blink. For the first time I felt uncomfortable in her yard. I did nod, thinking she was waiting for I-man to confirm that I did indeed remember, but her stillness went on. 'I told yuh how the city come and take her yute from her round bout a month later?' she say eventually, and she look straight at I-man; though not in the eye, more in the miggle of I face, straight at I&I broad nose. 'City don't come unless them call, Jabari,' she say.

'How yuh mean?'

'City don't come unless them call.'

'Yuh call them?' I ax, open-mouth, and she nod. 'Bloodfire, Cedella know?'

'Maybe – might have been what she was so upset bout when we went and visit her. Cedella don't need no more reason to be upset anyway, so I don't know what she knows, or what she think she knows, but if she find out, so be it: I stand by what I did.'

'Yuh stand by it?'

'I condemn a woman who I call my bredrin to childlessness, and at the same time, condemn Irie and the rest of Cedella pickney to a life without knowing them birth mother. Trust me, I knew exactly what I was doing.' She reach for a liquor cup that wasn't there. 'I need a drink, man,' she say, but she made no attempt to rise up.

'I did it, and I stand by it, but it wasn't easy. If yuh don't bring the bag back to Levi, then yuh betraying him, but if the situation feel wrong inna yuh stomach: then it wrong. And maybe I'm only speaking to myself, but I think that's reason enough to make up yuh mind. Whatever yuh decide, yuh affi decide what yuh think yuh can best live with for the next ten, twenty, thirty years.' She rose with her hands pon her knees and an ache and a stiffness. Soon as she stand, one hand flew to the small of her back and the other to her forehead; she wipe away the spots of sweat that had gather together overneath the hot reading light. 'Look at Angela,' she say. 'Me tell her not to do it, but she went ahead anyway because she her own woman and she make the choice she think she can best live with. When yuh stand in front of God, Jabari, yuh'll stand alone, my yute.' She held I eye until I drop it. 'It's been a long day,' she say. She come over and kiss I-man twice on the cheek. 'I'm gone to my bed. Yuh can look a food inna the fridge, I don't know how much of it is ital, but banana and them things there inna bowl by the sink.'

'Wait, Joyce?'

'Mmh?'

'Say yuh had a yute – I know yuh don't, but say yuh did – and say Jah ax yuh to kill yuh yute, what would you do?'

She blew a raspberry with her mouth and laugh, the back of her wrist leant on her hip. 'What stupidness yuh a ax me, yute?'

'Abraham and Isaac, in the Bible. God ax him to kill Isaac.'

She kiss her teeth. 'I'd tell God fi suck out, bredda. Goodnight, Jabari.' I went to pick up the boxer bag, but she stop I. 'Where yuh going, my yute? Back to yuh daddy?'

'To the allotments. I'm gonna stay there tonight while I think this out.'

'Shut up, man. Go sleep pon the sofa,' she say, and I was bout to protest when she went into another room and return with a duvet. For a second I thought bout stepping into the cold but quickly, I thank Joyce for her kindness.

205

13

I lay in the dark, awake for far longer than I did intend, but sleep wouldn't find I no matter what. I think back to the day before, when I could hear Miss Nefertari with Irie, and how happy she'd been to spend time with the likkle one, which took I&I back even further, to the time when Miss Nefertari and I had been close, when her yard seem like the whole world and our routine consist of haircare and singing to the radio, and tending to Pretty in the back yard. I could never say which of the two was I favourite. Each time she sat down to do I&I hair, her white towels ready, her products inna line, Miss Nefertari would tell I to go and fetch a handful of hard-boil sweetie from the bowl atop the tray. I'd bring them back and she'd put a finger to her lips and make it a secret, even though it wasn't. She'd say we'd blame the goat if Ras Levi ax. I'd laugh and agree, even though I knew that Pretty wasn't allow inside the house, even though I thought Ras Levi would never notice.

We kept Pretty inna wooden hutch that Ras Levi had specially built. Miss Nefertari teach I-man all bout the different breed of dairy goat: the white, hornless Saanen and light brown Toggenburg; the Alpine and Lamancha and the short-hair Nubian – animals she knew from her parent's piece of land back home. Pretty was an Anglo-Nubian. We had wooden stumps for stools in the yard, and I would sit with a Casio stereo extension-cabled from the kitchen playing roots. Before Miss Nefertari milk her, she'd have I wash Pretty udder with warm water, and I-man would pat her dry with a clean dishtowel. 'It stimulate the milk,' Miss Nefertari say, in her low, rumbling voice, heavy like rain. 'If we treat Pretty with esteem, then she will give I&I the best milk possible.'

Anyone who know anything bout goat, know them milk from the right-hand side, so that's where Miss Nefertari would first sit, and I-man would stand feeding Pretty grain and alfalfa hay. Miss Nefertari would discard the first squirt drawn from each teat. She toss it from the bucket into the grass and let nature have its way. When she was finish with the one side, we would swap place and I-man milk the other. When done, I&I would set the container inna large pan of cold water to cool. I'd take a big stick and stir to hasten the chilling before we place it inna wide refrigerator we use to keep outside. It was always the same routine: Miss Nefertari would oil I scalp and keep I locs neat, then we'd milk Pretty, smooth her hair or change her bedding. In those days I wasn't yet holding Ras Levi by the hem. I wasn't following him up and down the country. It wasn't him who home-school I&I, it was Miss Nefertari. Ras Levi would take those trips alone, and him did spend him day there at the centre.

Back then him rarely said a word bout the time I did spend

with Miss Nefertari, till one afternoon when him come home from the centre and find her cutting the ends of I locs to keep them level. It wasn't new; it was something him had seen before. Usually, him would walk right past we inna the living room. This time, I caught sight of him in the hand-mirror Miss Nefertari use to show I-man the back of I head. Him never know I could see him, but him was stood in the doorway staring. I couldn't work out him expression, but I could see him mind at work. Miss Nefertari never notice; she was talking to I-man bout something trivial – something she knew I would want to hear. Ras Levi must've stood there a whole minute, unmoving, and when finally him did, it was with purpose. Him close the distance between we with a few stride and lift I-man to I feet. Miss Nefertari go to stop him, but him tell her to shut her mouth and stay inna the living room.

Him lead I to the backyard, where Pretty rose to come greet we – as she always did. She was round ninety pound then. Miss Nefertari said we'd affi take her to be bred again soon. We'd already certify her health with another neighbour who rear sheep in Jamaica, and we'd found another neighbour who had a buck, and pon the calendar we'd mark a date four month down the line. Them time there, all Miss Nefertari and I could talk bout was what we would name her kid – it was probably what she'd been talking bout when Ras Levi first come in. I'd made a miniature bedded box and had it ready by the back door. Miss Nefertari said I could feed him by bokkle this time – I'd been too small to bokkle-feed Pretty, and the first time she kidded, Ras Levi never let we keep it. Miss Nefertari said it would take I&I bout tree month to wean him from milk, to hay and grass, and after tree month I-man I could take him to show-and-tell at school, but that afternoon, when Ras Levi did come home, him press him cutlass inna I-man hand and had I cut open Pretty throat.

She was aware the whole time. Him never stun her. Her long eyelash did stay wide open, her eye trusting I-man only a moment ago. I couldn't bring the blade across her neck clean, I hand did falter and the cut weren't precise, so Ras Levi make I-man go over it again, and again. Then we did sit there, fada and son, with Pretty braying and bleeding into the grass, leg a kick, and Ras Levi tell I&I the story of how him come to be Rasta.

It was in the months after him did lose both of him parents that Ras Levi, then simply Marcus Browne, first come across Ras Ephrem Emmanuel. I papa was fourteen and wild then, being raise between him maternal nanny in Wood Hall and him paternal aunty in Gimme-me-bit, bout four hours' walk away. None of him people thought it necessary for him to attend school. Sometimes him did help him aunty husband with them trade, and other time him fish with him maternal grandfada, but them man were strong and silent, so Marcus would often escape and go barefoot adventuring.

This was how him meet Ras Ephrem Emmanuel, who was always sat outside him lonesome green-and-orange house in the hills somewhere between the two towns. Him did have a big piece of land behind and round the side of him yard where him did grow vegetable, and him closest neighbour was a shout away. The first time Marcus pass, the old man nod, so Marcus would nod back, and then, whenever Marcus was walking between him two family home, him change him route so that him pass the old man house, and the old man always nod, so Marcus would nod back. And when the man start to raise him hand, Marcus do the same, and soon the man became the source of much curiosity to the boy, because this was the first man him had ever seen with locs growing outta him head.

Marcus think bout the man when him fish and work him uncle land, before him sleep, and as him went bare-chest through the south Jamaica land. Him want fi know why him paint him yard so bright. Why him always a sit pon him stoop outside, in the same skinny wooden chair – why him never left him plot of land. Marcus ax the man in him family bout the man, but them never want know, so him ax him aunty them and him nanny, and them suck the wind through them teeth and call the man mad. Him ax them how long the man had been there, and no one couldn't tell him; him nanny guess a decade, him aunty suppose generation.

The next time Marcus did pass, him shout, 'Hail' in greeting, and Ras Ephrem reply, 'Ale is a ginger drink,' and Marcus never know why him find that so funny, but every time him would chortle and call, 'Hail' when him pass, and Ras Ephrem only ever respond in the same way. It became a game, and it went on for some months, with Marcus happy to let him imagination sate him curiosity. When one day, Ras Ephrem beckon him over, and so Marcus went, and him see the man more clearly – see that him face had wrinkle into sharp canyon and had been so affected by the world that a deep brownness, which only came from a life working in the sun, had sekkle in between the crack. Marcus later ax him aunty them bout the man face and them tell him, 'For one who eat so healthy to look so, that's how yuh know him older than time.'

'Older than time?' Marcus said, astounded.

'Older than, "In the beginning God create the heavens and the earth,"' them say.

The man had a full set of teeth, though them were brown in him mouth. Marcus ax him why him never see him with nobody, and him tell Marcus that him wife was there in the house. Marcus laugh. 'How come she never come outside?'

'Yuh want I&I to call her?'

'Who?'

'I&I.'

'Who that?'

'That is RastafarI language, the language of I: the first I is I-self, the second is the divine I; constant recognition of the Almighty-I, Jah. Yuh must always give Ises to Jah in everything yuh do.'

'Ises?'

'Praises.'

'Why yuh talk like that?'

'RastafarI reject the colonial way of talking this foreign tongue we force to talk.'

'Who name Jah, that who yuh call God?'

'So yuh call Him.'

'Why yuh hair like so, yuh never cut it?'

'Yuh know yuh Bible?'

'A likkle bit.'

'Yuh nah go church?'

'Them ban me from Sunday School.'

'Why them ban yuh?'

'Cos me lick somebody down.'

Ras Ephrem laugh. 'Why yuh lick him down for?'

'Cos him mad me.'

'Yuh know Samson?'

'Yeah man, me know Samson.'

'Strongest man to ever live?'

'Yeah man, me know him, man.'

'Yuh see what happen when him cut him hair? Him lose him power.' When him a talk, Ras Ephrem took out a ganja spliff and start fi smoke it. Marcus was spellbound. 'Yuh want some?' the man say.

'That's ganja, isn't it?'

'Yuh know it?'

'My nanny say only wockless people smoke it.'

Ras Ephrem Emmanuel threw back him head so and laugh. 'So them say. So them say, my yute. Yuh want some, anyway?' Marcus did, but him shake him head.

From then on Marcus would always stop at Ras Ephrem yard, and Ephrem would teach Marcus bout RastafarI and the white devils made by Satan, and Marcus would listen and learn, and when time came for him grandfada to shave him head with him razor Marcus refuse fi let the man take him power and him run from the house, and him family relent – because the boy had lost him parent. And it was round then that him declare himself a Ras and start going by the moniker Ras Levi. And this new, enlighten Ras Levi did look at the world with a fresh perspective, and him complain to Ras Ephrem bout everything him see wrong; the wear and tear of him grandfada fishing vessel and the knots in him uncle back from working next people land, and Ras Ephrem would surely place every fault at the feet of white people.

'Who create the imbalance which create the labour law, which make yuh parents march with the people them in the first place?'

'White people.'

'And who create the circumstance which mean people affi work just to work, rather than work so them can eat?'

'White people.'

Ras Ephrem would sit back in him chair, content, and him would smoke, and him continue listening to Levi complain for a whole year, when finally him ax him who the greatest man to ever live was, and by then Levi was well familiar with Ras Ephrem and him locs was almost adult, and him would come, daily, to sit at Ephrem feet, and so him say:

'His Imperial Majesty Haile Selassie-I the first.'

Ras Ephrem shake him head. 'Selassie-I divine, I'm axing yuh bout a man.'

'Samson?'

Again, Ras Ephrem shake him head. 'The best example of what a man should be is Abraham.' And given Levi truancy at Sunday School, him remind him of the story of the Binding of Isaac.

Now it came to pass after these things that God tested Abraham, and said to him, 'Abraham!' And he said, 'Here I am.' Then He said, 'Take now your son, your only *son* Isaac, whom you love, and go to the land of Moriah, and offer him there as a burnt offering on one of the mountains of which I shall tell you.' So Abraham rose early in the morning and saddled his donkey, and took two of his young man with him, and Isaac his son; and he split the wood for the burnt offering, and arose and went to the place of which God had told him. Then on the third day Abraham lifted his eyes and saw the place afar off. And Abraham said to his young man, 'Stay here with the donkey; the lad and I will go yonder and worship, and we will come back to you.' So Abraham took the wood of the burnt offering and laid *it* on Isaac his son; and he took the fire in his hand, and a knife, and the two of them went together. But Isaac spoke to Abraham his father and said, 'My father!' And he said, 'Here I am, my son.' Then he said, 'Look, the fire and the wood, but where *is* the lamb for a burnt offering?' And Abraham said, 'My son, God will provide for Himself the lamb for a burnt offering.' So the two of them went together. Then they came to the place of which God had told him. And Abraham built an altar there and placed the wood in order; and he bound Isaac his son and laid him on the altar, upon the wood. And Abraham stretched out his hand and took the knife to slay his son. But the Angel of the Lord called to him from heaven and said, 'Abraham, Abraham!' So he said, 'Here I am.' And He said, 'Do not lay your hand on the lad, or do anything to him; for now I know that you fear God, since you have not withheld your son, your only *son,* from Me.' Then Abraham lifted his eyes and looked, and there behind *him was* a ram caught fast in a thicket by its horns. So Abraham went and took the ram, and offered it up for a burnt offering instead of his son.

Once Ephrem finish reminding him, him explain that: 'The problem with this world is that our black leader, politician and lay preacher, don't carry the necessary conviction to rescue fi we people from the white man. Conviction, Levi, otherwise known as belief, otherwise known as faith, over-stand? Abraham is the best example of how much conviction is needed for any of we to serve the Almighty-I and lead our people from the white man vice-like hold over we. Jah know say I worry for those of we already in Gunmerica and England and Canada. I-self I have family in England. I worry how them can find a place of contentment and spirituality in the midst of Babylon wickedness.'

'Them never should've gone,' Levi say. 'Them should stay here.'

'England mash up Jamaica, then them invite them to come, what choice them have if them can't make a living here?'

'If them man there just focus on Jamaica and work toward building it up into something—' Him stop when him see him master picking him teeth with him fingernail.

'Leave Jamaica behind, boy,' Ras Ephrem say. Him find a piece of something and flick it way. 'There's nothing here for I&I, and there is other Rastas here already to tell the people that. Rather, somebody need fi travel there a England and bring the people the God-given message of RastafarI. Tell them that what Garvey say was right: only in Africa.'

At first Levi family did discourage the relationship between Levi and Ras Ephrem; them refuse to call him by him new name and did want him to cut him hair to look proper, so him could land a shop-front job, but eventually them see the positive influence Ephrem was having. Levi was no longer stealing away from the man in him family to run wild in the bushes, instead him did learn to be silent and long-suffering like them. So Levi nanny did call pon Ephrem, and the two had a one conversation. Afterward, she get up from where she was resting pon him gate and tell him that him wasn't fi have Levi round no ganja smoke, but that them could continue them friendship. So them did, and Levi start fi follow RastafarI openly, and, to him nanny dismay, him did start smoking herb, and after him made some money working with him uncle, and it did take him tree years, him manage to buy tree plane ticket for Heathrow: one for himself, one for Ras Ephrem and the other for Ras Ephrem wife.

Him present them to Ephrem one afternoon, who tell him fi go inside and ax him fi him wife blessing. And so, with some trepidation, because even after all this time this would be them first meeting, Ras Levi went inside and the house was perfect: the table was laid and cutlery and there wasn't a dustball to cause a sneeze, and after a minute of looking, Ras Levi find Ephrem wife in an urn on the mantel. When him come back outside him apologise for never thinking enough to ax after him lady health. 'I-man is Rasta,' Ras Ephrem say. 'I don't believe in death but in the reincarnation of the spirit: we are spiritual being having a physical experience. But I wife was a Christian lady. She never look at things the same way, so I must honour her request by keeping her ashes with I. She say she want fi keep an eye on I&I and make sure I&I don't marry no next woman.' Him laugh. 'What woman can I marry, old as I am? I have wrinkles older than most woman on this here likkle island. She was a funny lady, I lady was.' Him explain that if him took him wife to England she would never forgive him, and him was too old fi carry her to Ethiopia. So Ephrem tell Levi to go on without him, to do what Jah instruct him fi do, but to ensure that him follow Jah with the conviction of Abraham – him tell him, him should always be prepare fi lose what him most love.

Ras Levi did tell I the story as him took the machete from I hand and wipe Pretty blood pon him trouser leg until it was clean. Pretty shaking grew still and she was soon dead.

'Yuh see Jabari, the Bible give we instruction on how to live. It tell we story so that we can overstand what Jah want from I&I. That is why Haile Selassie-I upheld the Bible as the

Word of God: so that we might live by it. Yuh see Jabari: I'm Abraham, and as I son, yuh must be Isaac. I won't apologise for having yuh do that, Jabari,' him say, and beside him I hid I face so I could bawl freely without him judgement. 'I know yuh and Miss Nefertari did love that there animal, but I affi test yuh obedience to yuh fada, yuh overstand? Yuh conviction. God test Abraham by bringing him to the mountain of Moriah and having him sacrifice Isaac. I own conviction get test when Ras Ephrem, on behalf of the Almighty-I, did challenge I to come a England by I-self and spread the word and bring as much people back to Africa with I as humanly possible. It is I responsibility, as yuh fada, to find yuh a suitable test, yuh overstand? Yuh mama can only teach yuh so much.' Him ax that I rise from the steps and close Pretty eye, but I shook I head. Ras Levi said him wouldn't ax again, and him never raise him voice, but immediately I stood, as rigid and fragile as a wick.

'What bout the ram?' I ax, and him twitch. I was focusing on the wrong thing, but I couldn't help it. 'The ram in the story,' I continue. 'Is that why Pretty affi dead – cos she a the ram?'

'The ram is Jah mercy. But listen and learn, Jabari; Jah mercy only extend to those who are obedient.'

'So was Abraham really going to kill Isaac, sir?'

'Course,' Ras Levi say, and him was adamant. 'Abraham was a man who reach the uttermost level of faith and conviction. Abraham knew, more than any other man, that everything belong to the Almighty-I, because He is the creator.'

'What bout the Almighty-I?' I sniff. 'Was He actually going to make him do it?'

'Course. Look what the Almighty-I do to Sodom and Gomorrah, and even in mentioning that story: remember Abraham fought for the lives of those people, Jabari. Him argue with Jah and ax Him to spare the city if Him could find ten righteous people, but Him never, so Jah bring Him wrath down pon them. And yuh see, Jabari.' Ras Levi touch I chest. 'When yuh look at the two story side-by-side, yuh notice something.' Him voice was far-off, speaking as if him alone did have the secret to life. 'Abraham argue with the creator of the universe for the lives of the many, but when it came down to him son; him rise early in the morning and saddle him donkey without question. What that teach we, Jabari? It teach we that matters of the community mean more than what is personal.'

To I ear, Ras Levi words were muddy by the lifelessness in Pretty eye. At the time, and for most of I life since, I wasn't taken by Abraham conviction, nor with Jah wrath; instead, I forever wonder how Isaac felt, tie to the stone. I wonder how, after the knife did fall from the patriarch hand and him hug him son, how Isaac did console himself and continue to love him papa. As Ras Levi and I carry Pretty body to the butcher, I imagine Isaac convince himself that Abraham did love him – him only love Jah and him community more. I imagine him beat him emotion down with logic and deference.

Later that day, Ras Levi ban a then-mute Miss Nefertari from seeing to I hair altogether, him send I&I to secondary school in Southmead, had I-man join him pon him trip round the country, and the rupture between I mama and I was made permanent.

And it was on one of them there trip him explain how every black fada of a black yute, specially a black fada of a black boy living in England, had the same choice to make: either them could teach we how cruel a place the world was, or the world would, and the world was far harsher than they.

14

There came a great bang in the morning, much like there had been a bang when Denton arrive at the centre with news of Angela, except this bang was follow by nuff cry of 'Police!' as Babylon put them ram through the Mother Earth. I-man was still dress inna the same clothes from the night before, and it was so early that for a second, I couldn't tell if I was seeing the sun or the high yellow moon through the placket in Joyce slat. It took them a couple swing to open the door fully, and in that time I did grab the boxer bag, zip it close, and dash to the back window in Joyce bathroom. The window was small and frosted, but I could still see that there were more coppers in the alleyway. I wait until I heard glass in the front door break, once I'd heard the pigs charge in, and until I saw the beastmen who were waiting for we in the back alley to sweep inside as well. I open the window and manage to force the bag through, then I swung the bag onto the bin below, and it land neat, sitting as though it had always been there, and given the bag was worse for wear I figure there it would stay, unbothered, either until I went to fetch it, or the binmen did come and toss the money inna landfill and Jah make the decision for I-man and RastafarI never went home.

Joyce see what I did do. She come outta her bedroom in her bonnet and gown. She praise I-man quick thinking and tell I to wait on the sofa – not to make no trouble. We could hear them on the stairs. She turn I-man bout face and I run for the sofa. I reach it as a pig boot kick the living-room door from its hinge and it swung and slump to the side like a drunk. The coppers had on them helmet and face protector and them glove. Dress in the same pollution. Them baton drawn. Them forward in the flat with a ton of noise and aggravation. Them never ax who I was, or what I was doing there. Them never make no such enquiry. Them clap I-man in chain and turn I onto I stomach. Them rush to treat Joyce the same as I – regardless of her womanhood. She was standing inna the kitchen, waiting for them with a glass of water. It shatter against the floor when them did grab her, and lance her foot bottom. Them lay her next to I-man and search her person. Her chest spill from her dressing gown, and the lino floor was cold. Joyce never flinch. I shout for them to let her fix her gown, but them did leave it open still. Then them went through the rest of the place: into the bathroom where them rip her towel rack from the wall, her bedroom where them raid her drawer and threw so many of Joyce clothes into the corridor that their falling sound like the flight of bird, and finally them went inna the kitchen where them did find two pack of beer and claim she was serving liquor without a licence.

The bond was tight round I&I wrist. The copper who put

it on and read I rights had sent saliva from him mouth onto I face. Him sweat was in I&I clothes. I felt Joyce searching for I attention. Her chest was still out, ball and soft against the hard floor, but her two eye were cool enough to fall into and find calm.

The coppers haul we to our feet. Downstairs, we see that them kick the bin and spill burnt paper everywhere, that them topple the fat Buddha, tip the bookcase, and rip the mesh from the ceiling. The concrete ground was cover with ivy and fracture pot. I look to Joyce, I knew she had left the books and the plants them because she did think that even the coppers were above destroying them; still, when face with the destruction of her life work, I never see her show no upset.

Outside more coppers and a bully van wait for we. Them put I-man on I knee, and them was bout to do the same with Joyce when one of the pigs, the sergeant, point at two a him man and tell them fi take Joyce back upstairs so she could change. 'Show some class,' him say.

Frontline was empty, from where we were outside of the Mother, down to Portland Square. Empty except for us. Among the coppers was a colour pig. Tall and moustache with a wide forehead and hairy knuckle. Miss Clarke, the Mother neighbour, must've heard the noise and she did come outside. She was still in her frock and bonnet. She want to know what the fuss was bout, then she see I and her hand flew to her mouth. The sergeant step between we. The black copper put him arm round her and guide her home. The rest of the pigs stay stony-face overneath them visor. Them watch the road and ax the sergeant how long Joyce would be. One of them said them need fi get outta St Pauls as soon as possible, another agree that it wasn't the place to dwell.

It was six, the time of morning during the long mid-week, where the cleaner and the nurse and the security guard and the bouncer and the warehouse operator forward from them night shift. It was dark and cold nah backside, full of mist, and the people them was grouchy and full of ache. Them jobs were dead-end but them had plenty a mouth reliant pon them wage packet. Them bus would drop them pon City Road and Lower Ashley, and many of them would walk along Frontline, some straight home, them leg too tired fi do nothing but wilt. Others might stop at Mr Delbert in hope that him shop light might be on, and that him might let them in early, and that him might fire up him patty oven and give them a meal. Some check the Mother, if only for a likkle conversation with people who spoke the same language, specially if there had been a lock-in the night before so them could at least enjoy the silhouette of another shubeen them miss. And because Joyce a take her sweet time, it was these people who happen across the pigs them and the bully van and I-man in handcuff. So course, them stop, first two, then five, then ten. Soon them was equal to the coppers. Miss Clarke come back outside, arm with a rolling pin. I knew all of them face and them knew mine. The pigs never answer them question, them only check them shoulder, pray to whichever god them worship, and tell the people to let them go bout them business, but I was Ras Levi boy and St Pauls had suffer enough.

226

That's what Mr Hunt said: St Pauls suffer enough. Him was a working man Mr Hunt was, had himself a handful of yutes and tree job, and him was tall, and despite a large gut him hard work did keep him fit. The police never answer Mr Hunt neither, them only look at one another and finger them baton, them gait shifty, so Mr Hunt address him next question to I: 'Wahum, young man? Them put them hand pon you?' The coppers threaten him with arrest. Still him wouldn't let up, him tell another man to fetch Ras Levi and promise that someone would answer for this. The man him send set off running, and at mention of I&I papa I panic, and the sergeant plead for him man upstairs to hurry, and more and more of the community arrive. It wasn't just those coming from work now neither, it was soon those on them way to work, willing to risk them livelihood to see that the Mother and I were fine. There were more than forty people by the time Joyce and the pigs return. Joyce was now properly dress, and she wink at I-man as them put her pon her knee. Someone rouse Mr Delbert, who forward outside in him pinstripe and try feed I pieces of fruit and cracker, but a copper put a hand in the old man chest and shove him so hard that him would've fall if the people never catch him, and you should've seen the way them shout after that.

The people converge on the guilty officer and again the sergeant was force to step between them. Him pleading hand and lip did them best to placate, but the people were angry bout the unemployment rate, the housing, the bleb pon them elder feet, the harassment of them children and the state of them schooling. Mr Delbert threw him fruit in the sergeant face. The sergeant radio for back-up, and two panda car appear in seconds. The siren sound and the people them did affi move fi let them through, but them show them distaste by slapping the bonnet and roof as them pass. When them manage fi park, the people crowd the door so the coppers couldn't step from inside. The pigs watching Joyce and I couldn't reach them neither, and the panda cars were climb pon by the angriest of people and them did become beach whales: useless and fat.

Mr Hunt, Miss Clarke and Mr Delbert demand to hear the charge. The sergeant continue to do him best to soothe the tension, but word had spread to all four corner of St Pauls, and soon everybody knew the Mother Earth had been raided and the people were waking up from them bed and flooding into the streets. I worry what Ras Levi would do when him reach. I look for Makeda among the people but I couldn't find her. Irie wasn't eating nothing pon nobody shoulder. I had a terrible vision of them inna cell. I could see that Angela was still fresh on the people them mind, and I know that anyone who had seen Ras Levi since him release wouldn't have been able to sleep for thoughts of vengeance.

All it need was one person to crack.

Ras Joseph arrive before Ras Levi. Behind him I saw the people I'd known I whole life: man I'd chant with and woman who had hand I-man plates. With them arrival came Denton, who was far and away the most outrage. Denton and I had been search side-by-side many time before, our face pon the ground, pockmark with gravel. Him had seen the pigs hit I-man and I'd seen them hit him. It was nothing new to neither a we: but I could see him hand trembling – I realise him couldn't stand that I was alone.

The people split so the Rasta could march to the front, and the pigs did form a tighter ring round we. The two groups were within spitting distance when Denton snatch a copper baton and struck the man with it, and with that the Abeng sound and Mr Hunt and some woman from the Mother lurch forward and join Denton assault. In turn them was join by another five, then another ten, and not twenty seconds later, everybody was hitting the coppers with whatever them could find pon the street, and if them couldn't find nothing then them took the lid from nearby bin. The people pull the coppers from them panda car and beat them into the back room of the Mother. And when I was on I feet, still cuff, but back with the baying people, I heard the sergeant radio the station to report the beginning of a riot on Grosvenor Road.

More reinforcement did come running from the direction of Portland Square. I saw them as them jog along Frontline, arm with them baton, and the milk crate them had taken from people porch. Them had with them eight dog handler and came to a company of fourteen. The dog handler force the people to make way for them assault. The German shepherd leash was long and slack, and the chaos whip them inna deliration. The dogs them snap at the people heel and leg, and them barking never cease. Them handler threaten to let loose them, less we back way from the Mother, and the sight of so many pigs and the sharpness of the dog teeth went a way toward quelling the uproar.

Gradually, we took to the pavement opposite the Mother Earth and gather inside a triangular patch of grass, where the young boys them gather round I-man. Them congratulate the height of I chin, touch the cold metal of I imprisonment, and them engage in whisper conversation bout restarting the violence. Meanwhile, the elderly lament the destruction. And all I could think bout was fetching the pardna from behind the café, when I did see the baldhead, Ras Levi, arrive. Him come alone, and him must have been the only person who weren't watching the copper – I could tell him a look for I-man. I push away from him, deeper into the people, trying to figure a way of recovering the pardna without Ras Levi seeing I, trying to figure a way to free I hand.

I emotion raise, and I couldn't think for the sound of I heart-beat in I ear. I never know where Joyce was. I couldn't find Makeda. I saw the black copper still outside the Mother, him nose now bloody, him taut hand certain that we were him foe. I walk to the kerbside. The road between the people and the café no-mans-land. I felt somebody tug I shirt. It was Battersby, Miss Cornwall and Mr Henry bredrin. 'Don't do it, my boy,' him say. Him hand and voice were gentle. 'That's it now. Trouble will find yuh enough, no need to look for it.' But Christ was a revolutionary. I step inna the road. Battersby hand fell from I shirt. The pigs them bridle. The snout of them dog pique. Them eye flash first to I, then to the people behind, who were daring them to take I-man back into custody, and while them attention divert I swung the metal holding I&I into the closest copper, and just as the people follow Denton, and as them had follow Makeda in the Gardens, them did follow I-man too.

Finally, the pigs spirit broke and the Mother empty of uniform, and other than the odd punch thrown and feeble baton whack, them never make no proper attempt to fight back. Them turn tail as one and ran down Frontline, Ashley and the length of City Road, outnumber fifty to one, ever chase by the people of St Pauls.

The majority of the coppers dash fi the border at Brigstoke Road. Behind them the people dip into the open skip and bins and flung ammunition at them back. Some of the slower officers were chase up side roads and into alleyways and were beaten with sticks and the bottom of boots. Several officers threw them own missile, but guide by fear them only land astray and serve to further rile the crowd. On William Street two park panda car were set alight. On Denbigh Street four man corner a copper inna garden and broke a couple a him rib. The people march the police to the border where them did promptly scatter. The sergeant pled for mercy, but him was met only with threat and a barrage of stone, till two elder ensure him safe passage.

With him exit, St Pauls was free, and the people did lift them arm, and a number of them did remain at the border, whether intent on playing watchman, or in disbelief, I don't know. Others filter along City Road, jogging and running without purpose. A handful sought the various discard piece of police uniform and set them afire. Them did overturn and put a match to every panda car until any indication that the pigs had ever step foot in St Pauls was alight.

Long, lawless minutes, maybe even a couple hours pass, and the early March morning seem brighter than it had ever been, and would probably ever be again. Once them finish burning the uniform and the car, the people turn them attention to the shop whose owner live outside of St Pauls. To the bookie and the clothes shop and the car dealership and the post office, and if not for a group of elders guarding the chemist from where them did collect them prescription, them would've raze that too. That's when the people broke inna the bank and the building burnt, and it burnt the longest, and its smoke rose the highest, and that's when car full of strangers start fi arrive, punks and anarchists beckon by the absence of the law.

I seen Joyce in her shop, broom in hand, sweeping the entrails of plants and the remains of the day aside. Somehow she already manage fi get her cuffs off. She bent to collect a broken plate and stroke its keen edge. I never had no time to dally. I went behind the café to fetch the boxer bag. It was still there. I swung its strap over I shoulder, both hands holding its weight to I chest, lips praising the Almighty-I. I walk past Mr Delbert shop, but there was likkle need to look in – the rude-boys were stood outside the shopfront with the old man, and if anybody did come too close them would turn them away with them flick knife and baseball bat, and the boy with the snub nose was among them rank too, him hand bury in him pocket, him face serious.

One of them call I-man over, so I went, and him took hold of I two hand and look left and right, then him remove a Stanley knife from him jacket pocket and force it between the locking mechanism and the teeth. Him tighten the cuff and push pon the knife and the thing come loose.

'Blessings, bredda,' I tell him, stroking I wrist and surveying the chaos. Him shake him head as if to say, *no matter*, and pocket both him knife and the cuff them.

'What yuh have in yuh bag?' one rudeboy ax, but it was then I was certain I seen Irie across the green space, a hundred paces away, holding somebody afro, riding them shoulder – and it could've only been Makeda. I dash back into the fray without responding, but by time I reach the spot I thought I'd seen them, them was gone.

I scan up and down, but it was too ram. You only caught glimpse of people, as them did rush this way and that. As well as the Bristolians from other walks of the city, there came journalists streaming into St Pauls. Them did come with them camera crew and them microphone and them agenda. Them come as close to the Frontline as them dare to and interview anyone who never avoid them. The face the cameramen train pon were West Indian. Artfully, them did dodge the white face of the English who travel from the southern and northerly sides of the city to revel. I overheard one of them report that outta the fifty or so police officers who were originally sent into St Pauls, at least twenty of them were injure, nuff panda cars had been damage. Elsewhere, I was certain that the pigs were licking them wound and plotting. I was sure that even in

them apparent absence them would send plain-clothe opera-
tive into St Pauls, committing name and face to memory.
I knew the coppers would call them night-duty personnel into
action, as well as the pigs who had taken leave, the sickly, the
pigs who were off shift, the coppers from the neighbouring
county like Devon and Cornwall, and Gloucestershire and
Wiltshire. I knew it was only a matter of time before them did
come back, because them bank was burning and them shop
was being looted, and the area that was once the pride of the
slaving city was now entirely in West Indian hands.

I stumble down City Road, walking away from the Mother,
away from the bank, inna trance, more tired than anything
else.

'Watch out!' somebody cry from behind. 'Them back!'

It start as a ripple on the horizon, the people who cut
from the shops on Lower Ashley Road and filter down City
and Frontline, but soon it transform inna stampede: behind
them, six hundred coppers were slowly coming up the hill.
Everywhere the streets were emptying as the people hurry to
avoid the closing cordon. Kind locals shelter strangers along-
side whom them had been looting only minutes before, and
for those who kept them door lock, them garden become
reluctant sanctuary, and without warning, I spot Makeda and
Irie running from the pigs too.

I step in front of them path. 'Jabari!' Makeda say. She was
alive. Irie shook. Soon as the likkle girl see I-man she scramble
to be in I hold, so I hand Makeda the boxer bag and take her.
Makeda complain bout the weight of the bag, and Irie, with

her small Bristol accent, say something I never catch, before she bury herself in I chest. Makeda pull I-man in one strong embrace, and I swear all the emotion I had been holding onto for what seem like forever, felt to release. I check her shoulder; they were moving slowly, thoroughly, we still had time before the police did reach we. Not much time, but time still.

'Where yuh been, woman?' I ax, but she never hear because of the noise, so she bring her ear next to I mouth and I ax her again.

'I went to Enoch yard—'

'Yuh papa? But Joyce people—'

'Me know, me affi hide inna the attic when them did come. I just needed more time to think, yuh know?' She was talking to I-man but her head kept swivelling this way and that, trying to consume it all. I swear not one part of her was frighten. 'I agree with yuh, Jabari, what yuh say before: it don't matter what England say is a crime – it's bout making the right choice. We can't rely on something like the law to tell we that, not always – but sometimes it's right, yuh understand, Jabari? I'm gonna take Irie back.'

'What?' I said, and it was all too much. The uprising. I heart-beat. 'When?'

'Now, before the police catch we. I was bringing her here so yuh could say bye, but then me see all this.' She held I elbow. 'What happen, anyway?'

'Unzip the bag,' I tell her, one eye still pon the coppers them. She put her hand inside and feel through the cash same how Joyce did, like a parch man inna the desert testing the realness of oasis water. But as she whet her thirst, she look up and see Ras Levi walking amongst the people over I shoulder. She tell I-man fi turn. Shook, I did, and found him still some way down City Road, but I knew him would surely catch sight of I&I soon.

'Listen, Makeda,' I said, and I start backing away, toward the coppers them. Irie start fi cry. She hold out her hand to Makeda, but I couldn't give her back; Makeda couldn't carry both the pardna and Irie, and the pigs would be back soon. Better she was caught with a ton of legal money than a stolen child. Better that. 'I need yuh fi listen, OK?' I say, hurriedly. 'Joyce is in the Mother. I need yuh to bring her this money, tell her it's from I-man, tell her it's a gift and she can use it however she see fit, but tell her not to be flash, otherwise the other Ras will know something up, and tell her not to cut them out too, tell her to make sure them see some of the money, at least.'

'Jabari, where—'

'Listen, yuh affi go to the Mother, right now. Joyce is there.'

'Where yuh a take Irie? Jabari!' Makeda kept saying I name, wanting I-man to stop and explain, but I couldn't, and even then, I thought to I-self how there really wasn't nothing I could diss. I glance behind I-self and lock eye with Ras Levi and see him pick up him pace, so I ran. There was likkle coherence to the thoughts in I&I head. I two feet did smack against the ground. Irie hung on fi dear life. I ran past the children home, toward the bank, and from there it seem the whole city was on fire. Alarm bell a ring, and there weren't no clouds above, only smog. The early winter morning was no longer lit by the fire from the bank, but by the strengthening sun and the coppers search and headlights. Only the young punks and rudeboys did still linger fi dash stone, and bokkle, and bin lid, at the approaching beastman. The pigs snatch every one of them. Them bind them and held them on the side of the road. Them smack them head pon the roof of them car and fling them across them backseat. The pigs took them sweet time to replenish, and them was meaner for it. Them went through the bookie and capture the punk inside. Them clear the supermarket and the bike store. The car dealership had already empty before them arrive: car theft too serious a crime for most people to risk getting caught, but I saw the coppers smash wing mirrors that weren't already broken. I saw Denton with a couple boys from the centre. I saw them fighting the beastman. I saw Friday desperately beckoning Prince, the two a them running for the Gardens. Prince was bleeding from him head. In the distance, I heard the loud sound of a clap like gunfire. I seen Makeda cutting across Frontline to the Mother, with the boxer bag, and that's when Ras Levi grab I-man by the collar and demand to know where the money there.

Ras Levi.

Ras Levi.

Him completely ignore Irie, probably thinking her some local child I'd pick up amidst it all; him tell I-man that I'd fail him, that I'd fail RastafarI, the Almighty-I, and our pursuit of the Motherland. Him become so consume by him rage that him box I in the miggle of the street and I almost drop Irie. She start to bawl over loud. It was then him ax who baby she was and tell I-man fi left her behind. I held her tighter and him drag I back to Miss Nefertari yard – vowing to beat the truth of the pardna money from I mouth. I stumble after him. Him still holding I by the neck and cussing. And I don't know what words I offer him in return, but I know say I did apologise and beg for him mercy.

We heard a crash and several cries. Hot air hit we. Ras Levi never change him focus, but I turn and lift I head and see that the bank roof had collapse. I look back at the man who Ras Levi had become: him loclessness and fearful eye that went from person to person, still searching for RASTA. Finding him nowhere but seeing him in every face. And right then, I came to realise that Ras Levi spirit was broken. Jah hadn't told him nothing this time. The message given to him by the old Ras in Gimme-mi-bit never change – how could it when the people still needed so much? But, if him word in Miss Nefertari kitchen were true, if him would actually put I above the people, then I was still tempted to trust him.

I was torn.

The story wasn't finish. I want to ax him to done it. I never know I Bible well enough. I never know what Jah said to Isaac. Right then I want, more than anything, to know what him did say, what him instruction were for Isaac. The story only tell I&I what Jah tell Abraham. But what if, like Abraham was to God, Isaac conviction was test by him own obedience to him fada? And what if Abraham had later change him mind – regret that him had ever listen to Jah, saddle him donkey and climb

Moriah without question – and what if him change of heart was evidence of him broken conviction? What would happen then?

Then it would fall upon the son.

To our left, two man mug an elder; I felt Ras Levi grip slacken as him battle him urge fi help. I took the chance. Immediately, I shrug free of him hold and I ran with Irie toward the bank and the approaching police cordon beyond. I heard Ras Levi bawl out I name. I felt the wind on I neck. I wasn't thinking. It was then I was set upon by the coppers. I head rattle from the ground like two palm on a funde drum. Irie spill from I arm. From the ground I seen some pig snatch her up. I try fi grab her leg but she was gone, gone back to the Roskillys them. Them thought say them did catch I in the act, them thought say I would bawl again, but inside I did smile, because by keeping Ras Levi from the truth of the pardna, by keeping him from taking it back and abandoning him people, I was saving him.

I see Ras Levi run toward I. See him toss the people who block him path aside. The coppers struck I-man harder than them did in the Gardens, an open tone on two and a dampen strike on four, but inside I only smile, because finally, in that moment, I overstood everything. I knew why Ras Levi had press the cutlass inna I hand. There, in that moment, with I responsibility taken care of, with Makeda protected and Irie safe with the system what was raising her, I finally came to overstand the lesson. I was only sorry it had taken so long. I want to apologise, to talk to Ras Levi again. Tell him that it wasn't the people fault them weren't as convince as him, him shouldn't lose hope – them weren't as strong. Them weren't born back a Jamaica, them never know half the things him know, them was too confuse – too British. Them never have the root nor the wing him have: them only knew how to survive. I want to tell him that him was right to put the need of the people over I-man; that him was right to love I less, because really him was loving himself less too, putting himself pon the back-burner. Because we was one and the same. Abraham and Isaac. Fada and son. He was I and I was him. I&I together. It was what the Almighty-I want. Inside I did smile. I pray everybody would benefit from the pardna money, St Pauls would benefit – Joyce woman them, the Rastas, even the Day-by-Days; that Makeda would find a way fi visit Irie, that St Pauls would be there for the likkle girl whenever she was ready. I pray that St Pauls would speak bout what happen for years to come. That through it them would come to see the value in RastafarI. Them would know that Ras Levi had been right the whole time, and that was the ram: Pretty wasn't the ram – that was it. Jah mercy did stretch out its hand so I could redeem I papa in him momentary weakness.

The coppers stomp pon I head and it rattle from the ground. One, two. Two, four. And I smile as I sank.

You remember we were then taken to the pig station in the city together, you and I, Papa, and from the pig station to the dock, and from the dock you was ship up north and them take I to a prison in Wales, and in our wake St Pauls was punish with crack epidemics and pacification.

I pray that when these lines reach you, Papa, them find you in the best of health, that them show you how I see things them time there. I don't know if you did hear the same, but I've been told the hard drugs manufacture more violence among I&I; the unity is gone. I hear your self-policing has flown from the window; that them create a reliance on the liarsment that wasn't there when we was. I hear them flood the place with money now, but the people never see it. I hear them elect spokespeople the people never heard of too; misrepresentation has taken the new St Pauls nation. Papa, don't fret. We still there a England, but Jah still with we; Him people, and the message of your life will never dead, so long as I remain your son, Jabari.

Now, with the talking done, I will rise from I&I cot, scrawl Exodus 34:7 in the bottom corner, where a painter might put him signature, and sign the last piece of paper with:

For Ras Levi: a covenant of love.

Respect.

Jah. RastafarI.

About the Author

Moses McKenzie wrote his debut, *An Olive Grove in Ends*, at the age of twenty-one. The novel was listed as a Guardian Novel of the Year 2022 and shortlisted for the Writers' Guild Best First Novel Award 2023. He was named as one of *The Observer*'s 10 Must-Read Debut Novelists of 2022, and won the Soho House Breakthrough Writer Award in the same year. He is also the recipient of the 2023 Hawthornden Prize for imaginative prose. He is currently working on the TV adaptation of *An Olive Grove in Ends*. *Fast by the Horns* is his second novel.